100

Death Trail

Travelling west was never easy. Men, women and children endured the rough terrain, the heat, the cold, illness and, sometimes, Indians.

So, when sickness struck, and wagons had to be segregated, the danger was increased. There were always men ready to take advantage and Clem Watkins and his gang were ready to do just that.

Ardal Maloney, his wife Kate and two children, had left Ireland to seek out a new life in the West. Leaving behind them starvation, poverty and death, they came to the New World to start afresh.

But the senseless killing of women and children fired Ardal into seeking to avenge their deaths.

Death Trail

D.D. Lang

A Black Horse Western

ROBERT HALE

© D.D. Lang 2019
Published in Great Britain 2019

ISBN 978-0-7198-2882-9

The Crowood Press
The Stable Block
Crowood Lane
Ramsbury
Marlborough
Wiltshire SN8 2HR

www.bhwesterns.com

Robert Hale is an imprint
of The Crowood Press

Typeset by
Derek Doyle & Associates, Shaw Heath
Printed and bound in Great Britain by
4Bind Ltd, Stevenage, SG1 2XT

Dedicated to the last of my three younger brothers.
Kevin Paul Doyle. RIP.

CHAPTER ONE

The silence was deafening.

Slowly, the sun's rays spread eerie fingers through the mountains to reach the desert floor, painting cactus and sand with a blood-red light that crept remorselessly onwards towards the stricken man.

He felt the heat on his face first, a welcome relief after the freezing cold of the stark, moonless night air. He blinked, once, twice, and slowly opened one eye, then the other. He breathed deeply of the warming air, knowing that this hiatus was but brief. Soon the sun's relentless heat would be unbearable; the air almost too hot to inhale.

He lifted his head carefully, ran a rough tongue over his swollen, cracked lips, and coughed.

Blood bubbled and ran down his chin. The man lifted his arm and wiped it off on the back of a tattered, blood-caked sleeve.

Smoke still hung in the air from the shoot-out, the

thick cloying smell and taste of black powder. Memory was hazy, but gradually, inexorably, the horror returned.

The mental image of two days ago flashed behind tightly closed eyes. Everything came back in an instant.

The Maloney family, father Ardal, wife Kate and two sons, Kevin and Patrick, had left Ireland over four months ago. The voyage across the Atlantic Ocean to New York harbour had been arduous, to say the least. They were lucky that they didn't succumb to seasickness or any of the diseases that swept periodically through the ship.

Many didn't survive the journey.

But surviving the voyage was now the least of their problems. A new country awaited them, a hostile country full of unscrupulous men only too willing to relieve them of their meagre possessions.

Welcomed at last into the Irish community of New York, Ardal began to search out a wagon train to head west: to the new lands of bountiful soil, green pastures and cool, clear water, where he could prove up some government land, build a home and take care of his family.

His, and their, dream. The promise of the New World.

It didn't take Ardal long to locate the next wagon train west. Bert Henman, wagon boss, had a good reputation. A fair man, in his fifties, with a beer belly that had been carefully cultivated over the years. He was loud, brash and ruddy-faced, with a ginger beard that had never seen the inside of a barber's shop, and flaming hair to match. When he laughed, an infectious laughter, his giant frame shook like jelly; it was impossible not to laugh with him.

Fees paid, wagon bought, provisions sought and purchased and carefully stowed away, their adventure was about to begin.

On 16 August 1851, the train, comprising over 170 wagons, some 200 steers and 50 outriders, set off at dawn in a long, snake-like formation that took over two hours to pass by.

The ride was rough and uncomfortable on the wagon, and Kate and the two boys eased their limbs, as did many others, by walking beside it. The first day seemed the longest.

By noon the sun, at its zenith, burned down with an energy-sapping heat that affected both man and animal. Three camps were ringed up, one beside the other. Fires were lit, water boiled and soon the air was filled with the aroma of food. Scouts kept a look out for anyone likely to chance their hand on a quick raid, but they knew that with a wagon train this large that possibility was remote. But Bert Henman insisted they do what they were paid for.

The head scout, Arnie Robertson, a dour Scot who rarely smiled, the complete antithesis of Bert, rode on ahead a few miles to make sure the trail was safe and clear of any debris. A fallen tree could hold up a wagon train for half a day.

Meal break over, the fires were doused and weary bones began to reload the wagons and continue their journey until the sun set.

Day after endless day followed the same pattern. The only excitement to break the monotony of their slow progress was if a wheel broke, or the steers wandered.

The flat, featureless country didn't help to break the tedium. Evenings were spent building fires to burn all night, eating, having a restful smoke and making sure children didn't run off too far away from the campsite. Beyond the light of the fires and the oil lamps strung on the wagons, the land was pitch black.

At various campfires, a mouth organ would start a lamentful refrain, or a fiddle player would strike up a fancy tune. Most folk listened, but there was no dancing; people were too weary, their bodies abused by the climate, the ride of the wagons and the length of the day's travel.

After three weeks, the landscape changed. Mountains loomed in the distance. Bert Henman stressed that this was the most dangerous part of their journey, not counting the Indians, he added with a raucous belly laugh: no one so much as smiled at this news.

He told them the trail was narrow and twisting, and that each wagon must only carry the driver and any elderly, of which there were a few.

Everything changed as if a magic wand had swept across the sky.

The flat landscape was replaced by rocky outcrops and hillocks as they made a steady climb. The temperature began to drop dramatically, and those walking discarded parasols for heavy shawls and blankets for the children.

The progress of the train slowed too, as horses, mules and oxen tired on the gradients.

Up ahead, Ardal could see the lead wagons climb steadily: the trail of dirt and sand was now littered with smoothed out rocks with deep ruts slowing progress further. Worst of all, the wide trail started to narrow until the wagons had only a foot clearance either side.

The mountains were upon them, slowly at first, but as they headed west, steep walls of rock entombed the trail, a sepulchre feeling filled the air and men, women and children walked in silence behind and in front of the wagons.

Suddenly, on one side of the trail, a vast chasm appeared, a sheer drop of some 50ft opened up, the wagons slowed further and, even in the cold dank air, the drivers' faces showed sweat with the effort of concentrating on keeping their teams on the straight and narrow.

11

Tragedy struck quickly! Ahead, a horse reared and the driver tried in vain to control it, but its panic spread to its mate. There was nowhere for them to run: ahead were other wagons and people! It didn't stop them trying.

Ardal reined in as he heard the screams.

Then he saw the bodies floating through the air as if they were flying, but the screams echoed and reverberated. Ardal counted four; two women, one man and a child. Then, when they thought the horror had ended, the back left-hand wheel of the rogue wagon slipped over the edge, dragging both wagon and team backwards, down into the chasm. Ardal was sure he heard the animals scream as they, too, plunged to certain death.

Keeping his own reins tight in his fists, Ardal watched two oxen on his wagon, to see what reaction the chaos ahead might cause in them.

They stood placidly, hardly seeming to even breathe.

Kate climbed through the rear of the covered wagon, the boys hovered behind.

'What's happened?'

Ardal felt her hands on his broad shoulders, and caught the scent of her hair as he turned to face her.

'A wagon, ahead, just crashed over the side.'

'Oh my god! Was there. . . ?'

'Yes,' Ardal cut in. 'The horses panicked and had nowhere to go, I saw four people go over the edge before the wagon slipped backwards.'

Kate was silent.

'I should go see if I can help, at all,' Ardal said, 'but I won't leave the wagon.'

'Give me the reins, Ardal Maloney, I can manage them.' Kate climbed on to the driver's seat beside him.

Despite his fears, Ardal smiled at his wife. Her bright green eyes and red hair reflected what little light there was, and her skin, the colour of milk and silky smooth, seemed to glow.

'Go,' she said, and Ardal knew better than to argue.

'Kevin, Patrick,' Kate called out, 'stay at the rear of the wagon now boys.'

There was a muted response and Kate smiled at her husband. 'Go,' she said gently, her face lighting up with that same radiant smile that had captivated his heart over ten years earlier.

He kissed her gently on the cheek, pulled his Stetson on his head down as far as the mass of black hair would allow, and jumped to the ground.

Taking one last look at her, he smiled, turned and walked ahead.

Squeezing between the wagons Ardal reached the gap where the wagon had gone over the side. A small knot of silent watchers were peering over the edge looking for any sign of movement below.

There was none.

'We better check,' Ardal said, 'I'll go down.'

Ropes were brought and secured and Ardal tied one end around his waist. 'Lower me slowly, me boys,' he said with a fake grin.

He turned, his back to the chasm, and slowly stepped down. For the first time, Ardal was glad he wasn't wearing riding boots. The stout shoes he wore, with a small heel, enabled his footing to be sure.

Lower and lower he went; broken branches and scars on the rock face showed where the wagon had hit and bounced off.

Reaching the bottom, he signalled to relax the rope. Untying it, he took a deep breath.

He'd seen dead bodies before; the potato famine back home, the evictions, the starvation, the reason he'd left Ireland in the first place, had hardened him. But nothing could prepare him for the crushed and mutilated bodies of the two women he came across first.

There was no need to check for a pulse.

He found the man next, impaled on a small tree. He seemed to be balancing atop it. From his face, Ardal could see he hadn't died straight away.

The child had landed on her back and her face looked almost serene in comparison to the others, only the still-spreading pool of blood that surrounded her gave evidence of her violent death.

Of the wagon driver, there was no sign. The horses, two bays, were smashed to pulp and the wagon was upside down, and Ardal instinctively knew that there was no need to search further. There was nothing he could do here.

It took Ardal nearly two hours to gather enough rocks to cover the bodies. There was no hope of burying them any other way, and he couldn't just leave them there for the buzzards and other wild creatures to devour.

He said a silent prayer, picked up a Winchester that didn't look as if it had been damaged, and retied the rope around his waist.

'OK, I'm ready,' he shouted to the waiting men. The slow and arduous climb back up was completed safely.

As he stepped back on to the trail, Bert Henman was there to greet him. For once, a sombre expression on his face.

'I don't suppose any of 'em. . . .'

'No. I couldn't bury them properly, but I covered them with rocks as best I could,' Ardal said and, despite the cold air, wiped sweat from his brow.

'Hot damn,' Bert said and took his battered Stetson off and lowered his head. The rest of the small group followed suit.

In the minutes' silence, Ardal was sure that everyone else was thinking the same thing: It could have been our wagon that had gone over the edge!

Bert donned his Stetson. 'Ya did good down there, fella,' he said. 'But now we gotta move on up, can't camp out here fer the night.'

He slapped Ardal on the shoulder, turned and mounted his horse.

'Does anyone know who they were?' Ardal called out.

'Nope,' came an instant reply. 'They kept pretty much to themselves.'

Ardal sighed. Not even a marker to say who they were.

Wearily, Ardal made his way back to his own wagon.

'Did anyone survive?' Kate asked, a worried look on her face.

'No, I found them all. I did what I could, which was precious little.'

Kate took Ardal in her arms, there was no need for words.

She felt her husband shudder slightly, then Ardal raised his head, his eyes moist, as he said: 'No one even knew who they were. Not even a marker. They might as well never have existed.'

Kate held him tightly as their two sons looked on, their faces showing they didn't quite understand what was going on.

'Well, we'd better get ready to move on,' Ardal said as brightly as he could, reluctantly letting go of Kate with a smile.

'Come here you two,' he called to his sons. He gave them both a hug, thankful, and rather ashamed to think, *better the unknown family, than mine!*

He released his two sons, smiling brightly at them, to let them know that all was well.

'You boys ride in the back for a while, OK?' Ardal said.

'Sure Pa,' they replied almost in unison. They didn't ask why.

For the first time since landing in the country, he realized that life here was just as cheap as the land he'd left.

CHAPTER TWO

Shifting his body to relieve the pain in his back, the man tried to raise his head.

Pain shot through his body. He gritted his teeth, and lay still, his chest heaving with the exertion.

The throbbing of his heart slowed, and he lifted his head again. The landscape was bleakly beautiful: rolling sand dunes, some dotted with cactus, others with tumbleweed resting, waiting for the wind to send them on their way.

Memories flooded back, slowly at first. He remembered the mountains and, looking up, he realized this was no desert, just a clearing, surrounded by rock that began to change colour as the sun rose, casting deep shadows on the bright sand floor.

The sky was still a deep blue, puffy clouds moved slowly across his line of vision, too high in the sky to mean any chance of rain, he thought idly, as he licked his lips once more.

He glanced down at his chest. The bullet had hit him high up on the right-hand side, he felt it had gone straight through. He hoped it had.

The bleeding seemed to have stopped, but he was still short of breath. Raising his left hand, he saw for the first time, he was still holding the Winchester.

Despite the pain he felt, he grinned, a crooked, mocking grin, as he thought of the men he had killed.

Slowly, the wagons began to roll. There was an air of gloom as word was passed from wagon to wagon down the line and, like Chinese whispers, the details of the tragedy got wilder and wilder.

The air grew colder the higher they climbed and, gradually, a sense of well-being returned. Distant peaks came into view, snow-covered and higher than anything Ardal had ever experienced, but then, everything in this strange land was out of his experience.

The trail levelled out as they reached this first summit. Ahead, the mountain range seemed to go on forever. They began to descend, the ground, cold and hard and unforgiving, began to show signs of softer earth, giving the animals purchase, which they needed to stop the wagons rolling on. Ardal fought with the brake with one hand, jinking the reins with the other to keep the oxen moving.

Soon the air was filled with the smell of burning

leather and wood and the sounds of grating as brakes were applied.

Below, green showed, a verdant pasture, quite unexpected in this bleak grey area. He hoped that it would prove to be their campsite for the night as the sun, now hidden behind the distant mountains, was beginning to cast long shadows.

The trail began to widen, small shrubs and clumps of grass began to dot the sides of the trail and the slope became less steep. Kate and the two boys clambered on to the back of the wagon, tired after the day's walk.

'Will we stop soon do you think?' Kate asked.

'I surely do hope so,' Ardal replied, 'this bench doesn't get any softer!' He smiled at his wife, the love he felt for her as strong as ever.

Kate glanced into the back of the wagon, both boys were sound asleep.

Ahead, the wagon train began to slow and you could feel the sense of relief wash over the straggling group of wagons. A chance to stretch aching limbs, drink coffee and eat hot food.

The train was organized expertly into two tight circles, there not being the space for the usual three. Animals were fed and watered and corralled safely inside the circles, fires were lit and the nightly routine began once more.

The four men dismounted and peered into the dark

chasm at the scene of the wagon accident.

They'd been watching the wagon train for days now, waiting for stragglers that they knew from experience would lag behind the main body of the wagon train sooner or later.

Then they'd be right for the picking.

The accident was a bonus.

Gathering their ropes, two of the men, tar torches tucked into their gun-belts, began to descend the craggy rock face.

Although dark, the descent held no fear for them. Reaching the bottom, they lit the torches and surveyed the area.

'Looks like there's not much here,' Jed Manson said to his brother.

'Let's check the wagon first,' replied Harry.

The ten-foot high wagon was reduced to the width of the wooden box it was built on; about 3ft. Both axles, complete with shattered wheels, were nowhere to be seen. The horses were still bridled up and were a mash of blood and gore, and white bones poked through their shaggy haired bodies.

Harry handed Jed his torch, took out his Bowie knife and cut through the leather straps. The wagon lurched as the weight of the horses was released, leaving a small gap at the rear and along one side.

Jed carefully leant both torches against a rock and, together with Harry, they lifted the wagon, moving it to one side to reveal what was underneath.

A sack of flour, still intact, and a plethora of other dried goods was revealed, along with a side of bacon, salt pork, and jerky.

'Well it'll all come in handy,' Harry commented, almost to himself. 'Let's see what else we can find here.'

Both men lit their torches and began rummaging through the scattered remains.

Clothes, toys, a few dime novels, a Colt and holster that had seen better days, some boxes of ammunition, an axe, shovel and pick.

'Bingo!' Jed called out.

Handing his torch to Harry, Jed retrieved a tin box.

'Got a padlock on it! Goddamn!' Jed said.

'Shoot the damn thing off, jus' make sure you don't aim yer gun at the box!' Harry said.

Jed placed the box on a rock ledge and took out his handgun.

The shot, when it came, reverberated round the canyon with an ear-splitting roar. Small stones cascaded down the rock face behind them, showering both men with pebbles and dirt. The stench of black powder and the smoke from the gun lingered in the still early evening air.

A scampering and rustling to their left made both men turn, Harry took out his service Colt.

'Just a critter,' Jed said, the white of his teeth showing as he grinned.

Reholstering his sidearm, Jed knelt down and lifted the lid off the tin box.

'Well, lookee here!' a bigger grin filling his face. He pulled out a wad of bills and waved them at Harry.

'What ya got down there boys?' a voice boomed from above.

Clem Watkins, their accepted leader, was atop the chasm, rope in hand still, along with Marty Smith, the last member of the Watkins' gang.

'Seems we hit pay dirt, Clem,' Jed replied. He tossed the wad to Harry and went through the rest of the contents. Cheap jewellery, some letters and pictures of a happy couple dressed in fancy wedding gear.

'Must be over five hundred here,' Harry said. 'Gonna tie the dried goods to the rope, Clem,' Harry said.

The two men busied themselves grabbing as much as they could and tied them to the ropes that had lowered them.

'OK, haul away!' Jed yelled.

The goods disappeared into the darkness above them.

'OK, boys, ropes coming down,' Marty called out and, as if by magic, the thick ropes swung in front of them like dancing snakes in the air.

Tying themselves securely, the two men began their ascent. Using hands and feet to gain purchase, the climb up was harder than the descent.

Eventually, the two men reached the rocky wagon trail, sweaty, but excited.

'Let's see the wad,' Clem said without preamble.

Meekly, Harry handed over the bills. Clem quickly flicked through the money and grinned.

'Well ain't bad fer the first one,' he bellowed and his huge frame shook as he laughed. 'Vittles and greenbacks! What better way to start.' He walked to his horse and stashed the money in his saddle-bags. Marty secured the food to the pommels of the four horses.

'Let's camp, boys,' Clem said and patted the saddle-bags, 'got me some real good celebratin' whiskey here!'

The four men whooped and mounted up.

'We'll hole up overnight. Figure the train'll camp down in yonder pasture, we can keep an eye on 'em and bide our time.' Clem led the way off the trail and on to higher ground.

Spirits were high.

The evening meal was long over. Dishes washed and stacked, campfires stoked up for the night. The two boys were bedded down under the wagon, and Ardal and Kate relaxed in front of the flickering flames, staring at the night sky.

'Must be a million stars up there,' Ardal said. 'And to think they're the same ones we used to gaze at

24

back home.'

'Look!' Kate pointed, 'shooting stars! Make a wish!'

Ardal pulled Kate closer. 'I don't need to wish,' he said, 'my dreams have already come true.'

'You're a long way from the blarney stone, Ardal Mahoney, but I loves you for it anyway.' She smiled and returned his hug.

Their mood was rudely shattered by the sound of distant gunfire. Ardal immediately sat up and jumped to his feet, scanning the bleak darkness outside the ring of wagons. It was impossible to see anything; gazing into the campfire meant his night vision was nil.

All round the campsite, men were standing and staring into the distance, each one trying to pinpoint the direction of the shots.

Surrounded by mountains, the shots, though faint, echoed and reverberated, making it impossible to even guess from which direction they came.

'What do you think they were, Ardal?' Kate asked.

'I don't know,' he replied. 'They sounded far away, but. . . .'

'You don't think it's Indians?' Kate stood.

'I don't think so. From what I've learned, the Indian lands are still a way off to the west. Could be hunters I suppose.' Ardal stood still peering into the distance, his right hand resting on the butt of his Colt.

25

'You're looking more like a real cowboy every day,' Kate remarked with a smile.

Smiling, Ardal turned to her. 'Well, thank ya kindly ma'am.'

Silence reigned again, there were no more shots, but the sound of horses' hoofs could be heard. Minutes later, two scouts rode into the camp.

'Everything OK here?' one of the men asked.

'Yes,' Ardal replied. 'Seems the shots were far away.'

'Yeah we figured that too,' a scout replied. 'No sign of trouble at the other campsite either. Keep your wits about you, we'll be on lookout for the rest of the night.'

'Goddammit! Quit that shootin',' Clem Watkins yelled. 'You wanna tell the whole world we're here?'

Marty, Jed and Harry holstered their six-guns and, shamefacedly, sat down by the campfire.

'Was jus' whooping it up, Clem,' Harry said. 'We got plen'y o' time fer that later. That train ain't that far away, no need to advertise!'

Clem took a swig from the whiskey bottle and passed it over. 'Still, ain't a bad haul, considerin',' he grinned.

The bottle went from mouth to mouth until it was empty, then Clem reached into his saddle-bag and brought out another.

'Now afore I open this I want no more whoopin', you got that?' Clem said.

'Sure boss, you got it,' they answered. They would have sold their own grandmothers to get at the whiskey.

'OK, one sip apiece, then we bed down. Marty, you take first watch.'

'Watch fer what?' Marty began to complain.

'That there wagon train has scouts, an' from what I heard, that trail boss, Bert Henman, is good at what he does. Those shots jus' might git him to figurin' on sending some o' those boys out to take a look-see. Ya git my drift?'

'Jeez! Boss! Why's it always me has to take first watch?'

'Cos I says so, that's why. Now you boys git to sleepin'. Wake me in two hours Marty and I'll relieve ya. Savvy?'

Marty merely muttered under his breath as he rose and grabbed his Winchester. He pulled his coat tight around him, dragging the string he used as a belt from a pocket and securing it tightly.

'And no fallin' asleep, Marty!' Clem warned.

'Sure, sure thing, boss.'

The three men wrapped themselves in their bed rolls as close to the campfire as they could get, as Marty wandered off to find a good vantage point, muttering all the way.

Dawn broke after an uneventful night.

Even before the sun rose, there was movement in

both camps, fires were stoked up, water put on to boil, and in what seemed like a few minutes, the aroma of coffee filled the air.

Fresh fruit and vegetables were in short supply now and were used sparingly for the evening meals only. Breakfast consisted of beans and bacon, mopped up with bread and washed down with coffee.

Animals were fed and watered, and while the womenfolk cleared away pots and pans and stowed them back in the wagons, the men hitched up mules, horses and oxen.

Within an hour, Bert Henman was calling out the time-honoured signal: 'Wagons! Roll!'

Slowly, the two camps uncoiled, amid much whistling, shouting and cursing, and formed once more into the long, winding train.

The descent from the first mountain range went steadily, the smell of burning wood and leather smoke filled the air as brakes were again constantly applied.

Yells of *Whoa!* rent the air as drivers hauled rein to avoid collision and slow down the animals.

The midday halt came and went; there was nowhere to stop on the narrow trail, they would have to wait until they reached the next valley. Women and children, walking as usual to ease their aching limbs from the bumping and grinding of the wagons, doled water out to their husbands and sliced cooked ham and pickles to ward off hunger until they

28

stopped for the night.

It was late afternoon when news began to filter through that illness had broken out towards the rear of the train. No one was sure yet what it was, but three young children, from two different wagons, were running a high fever. Disease out here, apart from Indians and bandits, was the worst news they could hear. Smallpox? Malaria? Rumours abounded, getting worse and worse the further along the train they went.

As the trail reached a valley and was able to circle up, the two suspect wagons were set apart.

'I'm sorry folks,' Bert Henman explained. 'But you gotta keep away from the main train fer a whiles. We gotta find out what ails your young 'uns. Can't afford no epidemic out here.' Bert removed his battered Stetson and wiped his forehead and the hat band with a cloth that looked as old as he was.

'I sent some boys around the camp to see if'n we got a doc or a nurse or anyone with some nous on these here things. I'll get back to you soon.' Bert pulled his hat back on. 'Don't worry, the scouts'll keep an eye on you overnight, but keep your eyes an' ears open, OK?'

Numbly, the stricken families nodded. Worry and fear etched their faces, as they watched Bert Henman ride off back to the wagon train, which was now some 300 to 400 yards ahead of them. Not far, but out here in the wild lands, too far for comfort.

The two wagons parked in a V shape, animals tethered on the outside of the V, and they built a fire on the inside, the wagons shielding them from the worst of the winds.

The children were still in the throes of a fever with no sign of it abating.

Water boiling, the womenfolk made chicken soup, the cure-all food, while their husbands mopped the sweating brows of their children in the wagons.

None of the children could eat, all they took were sips of tepid water, their delirium passing as they drifted into troubled sleep.

The sun sank with alarming speed and the night sky darkened to an impenetrable blackness that seemed to stifle any sound. The wind dropped.

The lanterns inside the wagons showed ghostly cameos through the canvas tops as mothers tended sleeping babes.

An eerie silence ensued.

'Seems we got stragglers, Clem,' Harry Manson said as he lowered the army issue telescope. 'Two wagons. Can see the lights burning clear as day.'

'Let me looksee,' Clem said, shifting his huge frame away from the campfire.

'Well, well,' he said, a grin revealing blackened teeth. 'Seems we got another early pay-day, boys. Harry, I want you to keep watch, I wanna know when, and if, them there scouts come on back a'checkin' 'em out, you hear?'

'Sure thing, boss. We gonna take 'em?'

'All in good time, Harry, all in good time. I reckon we grab some shut-eye. You wake me in two hours, by then we'll know if they're gettin' reg'lar checks and we can plan our attack.'

'How far behind are they, boss?' Jed asked, idly poking the campfire with a stick.

' 'Bout, three, four hundred yards, I figure. Cain't rightly tell from way up here,' Harry replied.

Standing and stretching, Marty Smith grinned as he pulled out a Bowie knife, kept in a scabbard on his left hip. 'Sounds like work fer my boy,' he said as he ran his thumb along the cruel blade.

'You'll get your fun, Marty,' Clem said returning his grin. 'Now get some sleep, if this pans out, I figure we go on in in the early hours, while they's all asleep.'

Silently, the three men clambered under their bed rolls; each of them grinning silently, excitement and greed and blood lust in equal amounts filled their minds.

CHAPTER THREE

'Boss! Boss, wake up.'

Clem Watkins sat bolt upright, six-gun already in his hand.

'What the—'

'It's me Harry. Them scouts ain't been around at all. Both wagons're in darkness, and it's been three hours now!'

'Goddamn! I tole you to wake me in two hours!'

'Was making sure, Clem. Didn't seen much sense in waking ya afore I was sure,' Harry said, with a hangdog expression.

'Ya did right, Harry. Wake Jed and Marty up.'

Harry stood and walked to the other side of the campfire, roughly kicking the two sleeping bodies.

'Shit, man! That hurt some!' Jed yelled, rubbing his side.

'You do that agin, Harry, and I'll slice ya from ear to ear!' Marty stood, the Bowie's blade gleaming in the dying light of the campfire.

Harry looked from the knife to Marty's face, and knew the man was not fooling!

'OK, OK, calm it down, boys. Time to get goin'. Harry, here, says there ain't been no scouts around since the wagons bedded down. Now here's what I figure.' Clem began to outline what they were going to do.

'I want no gunplay, is that clear?'

The three men nodded mutely.

'We split into two groups, two men per wagon, got that?'

Again they nodded.

'Harry, you come with me, Jed you team up with Marty. We got surprise on our side. Take care o' them folks quietly. Men first, then the wimmin. Got that?'

'Sure, Clem, same's we always do, let's just get goin',' Marty said, his impatience showing. 'Then I can git back to sleepin'!'

'Right, Marty and Jed, you take the far wagon. I want ya to circle down to the right. Me and Harry'll circle to the left. When we git to the wagons, I'll signal and we go in. Right?'

'Yeah, yeah, let's do it,' Marty said, his knife still held in his right hand.

Clem looked at the three men. 'OK, grab them empty saddle-bags, we take what we can carry.' He took a deep breath, motioned towards Harry, and they set off.

33

'Come on, boy,' Marty said to Jed. 'Let's get it over with.'

'I tole you, Marty, don't call me boy!'

Marty snorted, but didn't answer.

The climb down the mountainside was at least a half-mile. There was no moon, so progress was slow and steady. But the men were in no particular hurry. Better to get there safe and sound than not at all.

Thirty minutes later, Clem and Harry reached the nearside wagon. They hunkered down less than 20ft away, peering into the darkness on the other side of the camp for signs of Marty and Jed. The only light came from the dying campfire, set between the two wagons.

Within minutes, Clem saw a bright flash.

Marty, having reached the same point at the second wagon, turned the blade of his Bowie to reflect what little light there was. It was a trick he had used often before on such raids.

Clem smiled, and made a good impression of a coyote's howl.

'Come on, Harry, nice'n easy now.'

In a well-rehearsed move, both sets of men advanced towards the wagons, careful not to step on any twigs that might give them away.

But unbeknown to the four men, the coyote howl had woken up Jim McCarthy, who was sleeping under the furthest wagon. Slowly and carefully, he reached for his handgun, a brand new .36 Navy Colt, which had yet to be fired.

With shaking hands, he thumbed back the hammer and gripped the butt tightly. He watched as two men, both with knives drawn, crept towards him.

He squeezed off the trigger.

'Jeez!' Jed leapt backwards as if hit by a sledge-hammer.

From the resulting muzzle flash, Marty hurled the Bowie into the darkness. Such was the force and power, the blade took Jim in the head, piercing his skull. Jim McCarthy died instantly.

Clem and Harry gave up all pretence of stealth and rushed the first wagon.

Sleepy-eyed, Ted Williams and his wife Martha were sitting upright as Clem burst through the canvas flap. Ted went for his gun, but was far too late, Clem's knife thrust savagely into his chest. Martha froze as Harry grabbed her hair, yanked her head back and slit her throat.

Blood pumped everywhere, soaking everyone. Her gargled screams muted and died in her open throat.

Their two children slept on.

At the same time, Marty burst into the other wagon. Alice Williams stared back at him with the biggest, bluest eyes Marty had ever seen.

Filled with bloodlust as he was, Marty hesitated. Then he stopped.

'Don't make a sound, ma'am,' he said thickly, 'jus' hand over your valuables an' I'll leave you be.'

Still staring, Alice's eyes moved to the far end of the wagon.

Marty saw the strongbox.

'Thank you, ma'am,' Marty said. He even tipped his hat, flashing a smile as he grabbed the strongbox.

'Stay put, ma'am. Don't leave this wagon, OK?'

Mutely, Alice nodded. She glanced towards her small son, Ben, as he slept soundly.

Taking one last look at the woman, he grabbed the strongbox and backed out of the wagon.

Jed was too busy cussing to care by now. The slug had taken him high up in the thigh; just a flesh wound, but it stung to high hell and back. Marty joined him.

'You OK, pard?' Marty asked.

''Course I ain't OK! Goddamn it to hell! You get that sonuvva?'

'Sure I did. Jus' gonna get ma knife, I'll be back for ya, stay loose.'

'Loose? I got a goddamn hunka flesh knocked off ma leg, fer Chris'sakes!'

'You'll live.' Marty left to get his knife.

He found Ted Williams, eyes wide open, with his Bowie almost buried to the hilt. It took him a good five minutes to prise it free. Wiping it on the dead man's shirt, he grinned, then thought of the beauty in the wagon above. He relieved the dead man of his Navy Colt and, sighing, he returned to Jed.

'Come on, let's get outta here,' Marty said, helping

36

Jed to his feet.

'Jeez!' Jed pointed behind Marty.

Marty turned to see the other wagon ablaze. Harry, standing behind it and lit by the flames, was grinning like an idiot.

'Shit, the main train'll see that. Quick, let's vamoose, pronto!'

Dragging Jed along, Marty headed towards Clem and Harry.

'What the hell you torch the wagon for?' Clem was shouting at Harry and cuffed him around the head.

Harry's eyes were still blazing, he hardly seemed to hear or even feel Clem.

'Dang fool!' Marty said as they reached the other two men.

Harry went for his gun, but Marty was quicker, his knife already drawing a trickle of blood from Harry's neck.

'Go ahead, punk, draw.' The tone of Marty's voice was enough to chill the dead.

'Cut it out you, two! Let's get outta here afore the whole dang train arrives!' Clem started to head back to the hills, followed by Jed and Marty, with Harry bringing up the rear.

Harry was listening to the screams that slowly died from inside the blazing wagon.

Arnie Robertson was riding the far perimeter to the north of the wagon train. He'd slept little that night, having an uneasy feeling in his gut.

He heard a gunshot.

Reining in, he listened, waiting for more gunshots, but none came. The sound had echoed, making direction almost impossible to even guess.

Five minutes later, the direction was obvious.

To the south, sparks rose into the air, followed by exploding ammunition.

Digging his spurs in, he urged his mount forward, regardless of terrain. It took him ten minutes at full gallop to reach the site of the blaze. By which time there was nothing he could do. The wagon had been reduced to ash. One wheel still stood, resting on a broken axle, and the flames had died down. All that burned now was dry goods, and something else.

Robertson sniffed the air. He recognized that smell.

Burning flesh.

'Good God Almighty!' he said aloud.

He turned to the other wagon, which miraculously seemed untouched by the conflagration.

Dismounting and ground-hitching his horse, Arnie ran across and opened the back-flap.

Sitting there, blue eyes staring, sat a woman. Beside her a small child, sleeping, Arnie hoped.

'Ma'am?' Arnie clambered aboard, removing his hat. 'Ma'am? Are you OK?'

The same blue eyes stared, unblinking, straight through Arnie Robertson, seeing nothing.

Outside, horses' hoofs sounded and shouting men's voices filled the air.

Bert Henman, the wagon boss, had been drinking coffee with Ardal Maloney when they'd heard the gunshot.

As with Arnie, they had no idea of the direction of the shots but, unlike Arnie, their night vision was impaired by the glow of the blazing campfire they were staring into, so it took them longer to see the flames and sparks rising into the air.

'Hold it right there, mister,' Bert's gruff voice commanded.

'Hold your horses, Bert,' Arnie replied. 'I jus' got here myself.'

Bert holstered his weapon and tipped his hat back.

'What the hell's goin' on here, Arnie?'

'Damned if I know! This lady here seems a mite, er, well I dunno.'

Both men turned to look back at Alice, who hadn't moved a muscle.

'Seen her man?' Bert asked.

'Nope.'

'I'll take a look around,' Bert said.

'Ma'am? Ma'am? Are you hurt at all?' Arnie asked, knowing he would get no answer.

He didn't.

Ardal Maloney clambered aboard the wagon. 'Bert said we should get these two outta here, and back to safety.'

39

'Well we can try,' Arnie replied.

Ardal moved towards the small child and felt her forehead.

'Fever seems to have broken,' he said to Arnie.

'OK, you take her, I'll take the woman.'

As Ardal lifted the small bundle, a blood-curdling scream emitted from the woman's mouth.

'It's OK, ma'am. You're safe with us, come along now, everything's gonna be OK,' Arnie said soothingly.

'Knife!' the woman screamed. 'Knife!'

'It's OK, ma'am, you're safe now, come along with me.' Arnie backed out of the wagon, holding Alice's hands. She followed him lamely.

'I'll take 'em to my wagon,' Ardal said, 'we'll take care of them.'

'I found her husband,' Bert said, joining the other two men. 'He's under the wagon. Don't let the woman see.'

Ardal had placed the child near the dying embers of the campfire, while he hitched up the mules to the wagon. Arnie sat the woman down by her child.

'Give me a hand here, Arnie,' Bert said.

Both men dragged the dead Ted Williams from beneath his wagon.

'We'll wait till Arnie takes those two off, then bury him here.'

Arnie knelt by the body. 'Knife,' he said idly, remembering the one word the woman had uttered, 'straight through the head.' He covered the body.

With the mules hitched, Ardal led the woman and her daughter to the driver's bench at the front, covered them both with a blanket, and set the team in motion.

Bert and Arnie watched them go, before starting to look for a place to bury Ted Williams. Not an easy task in such a barren, rocky place.

'Any sign, Ardal?' Bert asked.

'Not a hope, too many wagons rolled past, but I'll check again at first light, though I don't hold out any hope!'

Meanwhile, Jed was gritting his teeth, as the four men made their way back to their hideout.

The pain in his leg was excruciating and he could feel the blood running down and filling his boot.

'Goddamn!' he cursed, as Marty half-led, half-dragged him up the steep path.

'I'll sort you when we get back to camp,' Marty said in a soft voice. 'Just keep your noise down, sound carries up here an' we don't want no posse heading this way yet awhiles.'

Ahead, Clem and Harry had reached the top of the climb and rested, placing the heavy strongboxes on the ground and relaxing their aching limbs.

'You ever do something like that again, and I'll kill you fer sure,' Clem turned to Harry. 'You completely loco?'

Harry, having calmed down now, realized his stupidity. 'Sorry, boss, I jus' don't know what got into me.'

'Well, whatever it was, it better ain't get into you again!' Clem spat. 'Didn't get time to do a proper search!'

Harry was silent.

Looking back down the gradient, Clem could make out the two figures of Jed and Marty, slowly making their way up.

'Come on,' Clem said roughly, 'let's get these boxes back to camp. We ain't got much time. We'd better head up higher into the mountains fer a while. Till things cool down.'

The climb back to their hideout took nearly three times as long as the descent but, once back, Clem and Harry set to forcing the strongboxes open, while Marty, cutting Jed's pants leg, took a look at the wound.

'Hell, ain't much,' he spat. 'Way you was carrying on I was expectin' to have to amputate!'

'Might not look much to you, smart ass, but it sure stings like crazy!' Jed retorted.

Marty went to his saddle-bags and brought out a short iron rod, one they'd used many times, but mainly for rebranding cattle!

'What the hell you got that out fer?' Jed became uneasy.

'You're bleedin' like a stuck pig, Jed. Gotta stop it

and seal the wound, else you'll get infected. Then I'd have to shoot you down like a dog.' Marty grinned, and it left Jed wondering about that!

They daren't risk building up the fire, but the embers still glowed red-hot as Marty stuck the iron into them. He sat down, reached for his tobacco pouch and rolled two cigarettes.

'Here, take a suck on this,' he handed one to Jed. 'Any of that whiskey left, Clem?'

'Yeah, over to my saddle-bag, there. Don't drink it all!' Clem was more interested in getting the boxes open.

'Ain't fer me,' Marty said, pulling out the iron and inspecting the tip. 'Not hot enough yet, Jed.'

Jed gulped. 'Go fetch that whiskey,' he said. 'I sure need a few slugs right now!'

Marty took a long pull on his cigarette, exhaled a cloud of blue-white smoke and, with a crooked grin on his face, walked across, slowly, too damn slowly to Jed's way of thinking, to Clem's saddle-bags.

'Son of a bitch,' Jed muttered, 'you're enjoying this, ain't ya?'

Marty merely smiled. 'Take a good few slugs, Jed, you're gonna need 'em.'

Jed grabbed the bottle, pulled the cork out with his teeth, and drank.

'Leave some in the bottle, Jed,' Marty said, 'I'm gonna need some.'

Pulling the branding iron from the fire, Marty

43

looked at the red tip. He searched for a piece of wood and handed it to Jed.

'OK, bite on this, don't make no loud noises!'

Jed glared at Marty: 'Son of a bitch!'

He clenched the wood between his teeth and glared at Marty. He knew it had to be done, but Marty was enjoying his agony.

Without waiting, Marty plunged the red-hot iron on the wound. Smoke and that sickly smell of burning human flesh filled his nostrils. Jed shuddered, groaned and snapped the wood in half. Blood trickled down his chin as splinters punctured his lips, tongue and gums!

He let out a shriek, more reminiscent of a woman, just as Marty slugged him into unconsciousness.

'I said, no noise,' Marty uttered in a flat tone.

Checking the wound, he saw that it had stopped the bleeding. Picking up the whiskey bottle, he poured a shot on to the gaping hole and then started to bind it up real tight. Then Marty, too, took a pull on the whiskey bottle, licked his lips and rolled another cigarette.

'How's them boxes?' he called across.

'Few hundred dollars. Usual crap, pictures, cheap jewellery, not enough yet to see us live the high life through winter. But a good haul,' Clem said.

'He fixed?' Harry asked, not really caring.

'He'll live,' Marty said.

'Soon as he comes round, we better saddle up and

vamoose,' Clem said. 'Kill that fire and we'll ditch these boxes someplace.'

Harry reached for his spade and began shovelling what earth there was on to the fire. Then he took a leak on it and a spiral of steam rose lazily into the air.

Clem and Harry loaded up the horses, then carried the now empty boxes and threw them into a gully.

Marty finished his quirly, rose to his feet and kicked Jed with the toe of his boot.

'Come on, we gotta high-tail it, pard,' he said.

Groggily, Jed opened one eye, a bolt of pain shooting through his head.

'Shit! What ya slug me for?'

'You was screamin' like a banshee,' Marty replied. 'Had to do something, else we'd a-had company fer sure.'

'Get mounted, boys,' Clem ordered. 'How's the leg?' he asked Jed.

'Don't know what hurts more, leg or head!'

Marty grinned, and helped Jed to his feet.

When all four were mounted, Clem led the way higher in the mountains. He figured they'd lie low for two, maybe three days, let the heat die down, then pick up the wagon train's trail again. The speed those things moved, Clem knew it wouldn't take long to catch them up.

And it wasn't as if they'd have to search for signs: there was only one trail, and Clem knew it like the back of his hand.

Feeling good, Clem walked on, his horse picking a careful path upwards. The night air was cold, but the wind had dropped and, overhead, the stars shone like bullet holes in a barn wall.

Yessirree, winter was gonna be high livin', he thought. Whiskey and women! What more could a man want. Well, maybe a fine cigar wouldn't go amiss either, he thought, and the crooked grin spread wider.

As he thought of the women, his loins burned in anticipation, but he quelled any more thoughts on that subject. A man could get awful lonely without female companionship.

Then he got back to matters in hand. Only three wagons so far, but nearly $1,000 in folding, and they could raise extra bucks with the jewellery and such.

Life sure was good, Clem smiled to himself.

CHAPTER FOUR

Daybreak.

Alice and her daughter had slept through the night. The little girl's fever was well and truly broken and colour had returned to her cheeks.

Ardal greeted Bert and Arnie as they rode up to his wagon.

'Going back over yonder,' Arnie said, 'see if I can find any sign. We gotta check the burned-out wagon, too.'

'I'll ride with you,' Ardal said.

The three men set off across the short distance to the still smouldering wagon.

Dismounting, Arnie knelt and looked at the ground. He could see nothing, the soil, what there was of it, was badly trampled; mules, horses, oxen, wagon-wheels and boot prints of all different shapes and sizes.

Arnie stood and circled the area, then stopped

suddenly. Kneeling, he rubbed dirt between his thumb and forefinger.

Blood.

He'd wondered about the shot he'd heard the night before. Figuring any robber would be quiet, seeing as how the wagon train was so close, now he knew where the shot had come from. Jim McCarthy had loosed off a shot and did some damage. A wry grin lit Arnie's face. That will slow 'em down, he thought, if he's still alive.

He searched around the blood-soaked area; kneel prints, and someone wearing high-heel riding boots! Unusual, he thought. Well there were two of 'em at least.

He followed a trail of two men, one limping, until they hit rock and the sign vanished. Then he spotted blood again, an intermittent trail of blood.

'Bert!' he called out, 'I found something here!'

'So've we, Arnie,' Bert called back. 'An' I wished we hadn't!'

Stopping, Arnie looked across to the other two men, then slowly made his way towards them.

Both Bert and Ardal had removed their Stetsons and were staring, open-mouthed, into the charred remains of the second wagon.

Ardal turned away and threw up.

'Jeez!' Arnie muttered, also removing his hat. He stared in horror at the bodies, black, fingers burned off, eyes gone. Four bodies: two obviously children.

'You think they were. . . .' Bert stopped.'

'Dead first? I dunno, Bert. I sure as hellfire hope so! Goddamn!'

Arnie studied the remains. Already the stench of death was filling his nostrils and he knew then for a fact that the two children had been alive. Their gaping mouths were evidence enough. He said nothing. Bile filled his throat and it took every ounce of strength not to throw up.

Forcing himself, he looked over at one of the adults, burned black, but obviously a woman. Kneeling, he peered at the corpse.

'This one's had her throat cut,' he said, standing and backing away. He hadn't the heart to look at the fourth victim.

Taking a deep breath, trying to lose the taste of death, he said: 'I found blood over by the other wagon. Drips of it head over that way,' he pointed.

'Seems McCarthy got one of them before he died. Two men for sure hit that wagon, and, I guess another two here. I reckon on four, maybe five men involved. One wounded now, or even dead mebbe.'

'Round up the boys, Arnie. Ardal? You OK?'

'Yeah, I guess,' Ardal murmured, though patently he was not!

'You up to helping bury these folk? I'll send some men over to help. I gotta get this train rolling.'

'Sure, yeah, I can manage, if you can send maybe one or two to help,' Ardal said, his voice thick with emotion. 'Can you get someone to take care of my wagon?' he added.

'Sure, no problem,' Bert said. 'Arnie, take ten men and track these no good, murdering scumbags down! I want their bodies brought back here so's folk can see 'em!' Bert spat heavily into the ground.

'On my way, Bert. I'll tell the rest of the scouts to spread out ahead and keep their eyes skinned, too.'

Arnie mounted up and rode off to form his posse.

'I'll send help over, Ardal. Sure 'preciate your help here.' Bert also mounted.

'Tell my wife will you, Bert. Tell her I'm OK and I'll catch up in a few hours, OK?'

'Sure, no worries, your family will be well looked after, don't fear.'

Pulling on the reins, Bert turned his horse and galloped back to the wagon train, where already, fires were being doused and gear stowed away ready for another day's arduous trek.

Left alone with his thoughts, Ardal couldn't stop staring at the charred remains and, try as he might, he was glad it wasn't *his* family.

Although the thought made him feel guilty, it wouldn't go away.

For the first time in his life, Ardal Maloney wished he smoked!

Sighing, and fighting back the bile that still threatened to fill his mouth, Ardal took the canteen from his pommel, swilled water around his mouth and spat it out. It tasted bitter, but then, Ardal thought, anything he put in his mouth on this day would be bitter.

Hanging the canteen back on his pommel, he took down first his spade, strapped to his bed roll, then he unsheathed his rifle.

A single-shot breech-loader, he hadn't fired the Sharps rifle yet, but the gunsmith had explained how it worked, how to load it, and assured him it was the finest, most modern firearm available.

So far Ardal had heeded the gunsmith's warning about keeping the linen cartridges dry. He had them wrapped in oilskin along with the cap locks.

The Sharps was comfortably heavy, business-like and felt good in his hands. It helped him take his mind off what he was about to do.

Back at the wagon train, Bert rode up to Kate's wagon.

'Where's Ardal,' she asked, a slight look of concern showed on her face.

'He's fine, ma'am,' Bert answered, allaying her fears. 'My chief scout found sign of the murdering robbers, so he's organizing a posse. Ardal's stayed back there to help with the buryin'. I'll get some men together to hitch up your horses and drive the wagon till Ardal returns, if'n that's OK with you, ma'am.'

Kate nodded, numbly.

'Now I gotta get these wagons rolling. We got

about another three, maybe four, weeks to clear this mountain range, an' we must do it afore the snow come, else we'll be stuck here come springtime.'

'I understand, Mr Henman,' Kate said quietly.

'An' call me Bert, ma'am, "Mr" don't hang too well with me,' he smiled.

'As long as you don't call me "ma'am",' Kate replied. 'I'm Kate.'

Bert tipped his battered Stetson, 'In that case, Kate it is.'

'Bert,' she said and smiled.

'I'll send a good man over, now don't you fret none.'

Tipping his Stetson again, Bert pulled rein and headed off. Arnie caught up with him as he reached the lead wagon.

'I got me nine men, Bert. I've reorganized the scouts, they know what to do and the cattle are tended. We aim to meet up with the train in five or six days, God willing. It'll take a lot of luck to track these critters down, so I gotta put a time limit on it, OK?'

'Sure, Arnie, I know you'll do your best. Good luck amigo.'

Bert didn't hang around. Once Arnie and his men had rode off, he turned to his number one, a grizzly old-timer named Red, who was also the cook. 'Ready?'

'Been ready for hours, seems like,' Red replied.

Bert ignored the old man.

'Wagons! Roll!' he hollered.

Now three wagons light, the huge convoy set off west once more.

'This'll do,' Clem said as they reached a small blind canyon. 'May only be one way out, but there's sure only one way in, too.'

The four men had ridden all night, now, as sun-up approached, weary in the saddle, they would have slept on a cactus patch.

Dismounting gingerly, Jed grabbed at his bed roll and long prairie coat. Within minutes he was asleep.

Harry and Marty gathered brush and wood and started up a fire; coffee was uppermost in their minds.

All three acted as if they hadn't a care in the world.

Two men Ardal didn't know arrived, armed with spades, tarpaulins and a pick axe. One, Morty Salmon as he introduced himself, took less than thirty seconds before he threw up at the sight of the gruesome scene.

' 'S OK,' Ardal said as the man mumbled an apology, 'I did that earlier.'

'Let's get this done,' the other man said, 'I don't want to leave my family too long. Not now.' He didn't bother introducing himself, so Ardal didn't either.

They started to dig in a patch of dirt till they

reached bedrock, the hole 3ft deep and 6ft wide. There was no way they could go deeper.

'We'll bury them all together,' Ardal said, and pile rocks atop, OK?'

The other two men nodded silently as they began to move the bodies.

'Aw shit!' Monty said looked down at one of the children. He retched violently, and Ardal helped to wrap the small body in a strip of tarpaulin. One by one, they wrapped the other three bodies and carried them reverently over to the shallow grave.

They rested, briefly. Not through exhaustion, but each man seemed to be thinking of their own wives and children.

Then they began to shovel dirt, the soil making an eerie sound as it hit the tarps. Slowly but surely, the bodies were covered. Then they began to pile rocks over the grave.

'That should keep any critters out,' Ardal said. He removed his hat. The other two followed suit.

'Lord,' Ardal began, 'take these poor folks under your wing and may they enjoy the eternal bliss of your love. May they rest in peace together. Amen.'

His throat filled as the three men stood silently for a moment, each lost in his own thoughts. They didn't even know the family's name.

'Thanks for your help,' Ardal then said and shook each man's hand. Silently, they rode away.

Ardal lingered. Thinking. A battle was going on

inside him that he found difficult to fight.

'Forgive me, Kate,' he said out loud. 'I've got to do this.'

He led his mount over to where Arnie had spotted the trail of blood. Then he sighted up the incline. Too steep to risk riding his horse, but he could lead it up, he thought.

Ardal was no tracker, he knew that; not much call for it back in Ireland. He almost smiled at that thought. Then he began the ascent. The blood drips made this part of the search easy. The man may not be dead, he thought, but he sure was losing blood.

His mount snickered, the steep rise was rocky and more than once the metal shoes slipped, tugging at the reins as Ardal led, but they made it to the top in one piece.

Pausing, Ardal studied the ground ahead. The man had obviously stopped here, too, the small pool of blood evidence to that fact. He hoped fervently the man suffered a long and lingering death.

Ardal mounted up and walked his horse on. He wondered how Arnie was doing with the posse and whether they would come this way or find some other route.

He reined to a halt. There in front of him was the remains of a campfire. He dismounted, the ashes were cold but he sniffed the site. Wood smoke was still lingering, so he figured this was where they were holed up. He confirmed this by noting the blood on the far side of the fire.

'Now what?' he said aloud. Looking round, he saw the tracks of horses. He had no idea how many, but their trail led upwards and slightly west. He followed, walking his mount and keeping his ears and eyes alert.

Several times he lost track of the trail, but always managed to see something to keep him in the right direction.

The path began to narrow and Ardal's eye, getting used to looking for the unseen, could pick out broken and bruised twigs where the horses had passed through. Concentrating so hard on what was near at hand, and congratulating himself for spotting these small signs, he failed to see smoke ahead.

Arnie had led the posse through the far side of the pass. He'd noted the steep rise the outlaws had taken and knew to try and ride that way was fraught with disaster. He knew that this trail would eventually bring them to the top of the rise and from there he hoped to pick up their trail.

This was not a place to gallop. The terrain was alternately rocky and soft going, an easy way for an animal to break a leg or throw a rider, so the pace was gentle. Arnie figured the outlaws would be hindered by their wounded *compadre*, if he wasn't already dead.

The nine men Arnie had with him were all experienced riders, had done the trail west many times and were a hardy bunch, he had every confidence in their ability.

Clem was arranging lookouts. The small canyon was ideal for a hidey-hole, he thought. Just one way in, which was easily covered. A small brook tricked down one rock face, enough water to last them in a siege, if it came to that. At the end of the canyon, enough concealed points for the lookouts to pick off any rider trying to get into the canyon.

He checked their vittles, enough to keep the four men fed for a month or more if need be. He was confident that the ammo they had, theirs and the ammo taken from the wagons, was more than enough.

Clem smiled.

'Harry, Marty, soon's we've eaten, stake out them rocks yonder, you get a good view of the entrance there. If'n they organize a posse, it'll be sooner rather than later they'll come a-riding in and we ain't made that much headway.'

'You expectin' 'em, boss?'

'Depends on the trail boss. He ain't gonna risk the safety of the many for too long, any amount of men he might send out will leave the wagon train vulnerable, so it's a poker game.

'If he sends out a posse, then they can only hunt us for a while. He won't risk men being away for too long,' Clem finished, then began rolling a cigarette.

'So we'll take it in turns to keep a lookout, anyone

heading this way will stick out like a whore on a pig's back.' Clem lit his cigarette, and leaned back on his saddle, completely relaxed.

'Beans an' bacon ready,' Harry called out. 'Marty can take first watch as I done the cooking, OK?'

'Sure,' Marty answered, 'fair enough.'

The three men ate quickly, while Jed slept on. They knew he'd lost a lot of blood, so they didn't bother waking him, but left some food for him for when he did wake.

Chow over with, Marty took his rifle and climbed the far end of the canyon. When he found a suitable place, overlooking the whole canyon and at least 300 yards of trail that led in, he waved to Clem, who signalled back.

'Right,' Clem said. 'Time for some shut-eye.'

He grabbed his bed roll and, using his saddle as a pillow, was asleep in seconds. Harry left the dishes and the remains of the beans and bacon for Jed, and followed Clem's example.

Pretty soon the only sounds coming from the canyon were the gentle cracklings of the campfire, and muffled snorts and snores of the sleeping men. Marty got himself comfortable, rolled a cigarette and kept alert, beady eyes on the canyon entrance.

The two men who had been on burial detail had returned to their respective families before reporting to Bert. They related their experiences and what they had seen, leaving most of the gruesome detail out, and pretty soon the whole wagon train was aware of what had happened.

Bert, riding the line up and down the train, was peppered with questions. He tried to allay their fears about Indians or gangs of outlaws stalking them, waiting to pick them off one by one, and telling the same story to each group or family that accosted him.

Some of the travellers seemed content with his answer, others kept their rifles and handguns ready – just in case. Worried expressions showed on mothers' faces and they attempted to smile in front of their children as if all was well in the world.

Although there was a mood of trepidation, there was also anger, as news of the two dead children reached their ears. Mothers kept their own close to them, almost all chose to ride in the backs of the bumping, grinding wagons rather than walk and risk any danger from an unseen enemy.

Bert Henman drew alongside Kate's wagon and was surprised to see the relief driver still there.

'Where the hell's Ardal?' he demanded of the man.

'Beats me boss. Ain't seen hide nor hair of him yet.'

Puzzled, Bert rode down the line till he came to Monty's wagon.

'Ardal not ride back with you?' he asked.

'No, we left him at the graveside, said he'd follow on.'

'Goddamnit!' Bert exploded. 'I hope he ain't done nothin' stupid!'

Turning in the saddle, he called to two outriders. 'Take a run back to the campsite and see if there's anyone there. Report back to me as soon as you can.'

'Sure thing, boss,' one of the men answered, and they wheeled their mounts around and galloped back.

'Hellfire!' Bert said under his breath.

'You think them outlaws got him, Mr Henman?' Monty asked.

'I don't know, I just hope he ain't on no vengeance drive and tryin' to hunt 'em down on his own. He's a good man, but a greenhorn hereabouts.'

Kate had heard the conversation between the relief driver and Bert Henman, and was filled with alarm.

She knew her husband. Knew what he was capable of.

She also knew what he was doing.

Clutching her children to her, she kept quiet and prayed.

Ardal rode on, still oblivious as to what awaited him ahead on the trail.

CHAPTER FIVE

Bert Henman had no option other than push on. There were too many lives at stake and he'd never had to winter out a wagon train before. He didn't intend this one to be the first.

Ahead, all that could be seen were mountains; range after range stretched out as far as the eye could see in a multitude of colours, ice-white on some of the taller peaks, grey, brown, green, yellow, orange and red where the sun hit.

Bert knew what dangers lay ahead. Apart from man-made mistakes, bad driving and impatience, there was also the natural enemy; mountain lions and bears being the obvious ones, but also cold. Bert had seen men freeze overnight. A few drinks too many in front of a campfire, then sleeping in a sleep they would never wake up from as the fires burned down. He'd warned people of this, but it still happened.

Then there was disease. Colds, flu and pneumonia always hit the elderly first and would sweep through the train in a matter of days. Worse than those was smallpox, dysentery and consumption; Bert had seen them all. With so many folks coming from so many places in the world, it was inevitable.

Fresh food was now running short, what vegetables there were limp and fruit soft, turning to mush, almost inedible. Dried goods would have to see them across the mountains till they reached a settlement or township. When they hit the Plains, traders would miraculously appear out of nowhere. Prices would be exorbitant, but Bert knew parents would buy to keep their young alive and as healthy as possible. Meat was aplenty; fresh, salted and on the hoof.

A moment's loss of concentration could shatter a wheel, delaying the train for hours. An overladen wagon could split axles, and even though spares were aplenty, the delays could prove fatal.

Now that Bert knew the train was being stalked, a fact he kept to himself for the time being, he could allow no stragglers. For whatever reason, whether it be disease or accident, the train had to keep together. If Arnie failed in his search for the murdering scum, Bert knew he would have to double the guard and maintain vigilance twenty-four hours a day.

As if the journey itself wasn't bad enough!

Bert led his horse to higher ground and looked

down at the snaking wagon train, his eyes moving from wagon to wagon.

He'd seen, over the past few weeks, the looks of excitement and anticipation turn to weariness and fear as the elements took their toll. Children who'd started the journey with happy, smiling, eager rosy faces were now sombre, quiet and pale.

Bert could see the energy and drive being dissipated. Time, he thought, for a shindig. Spirits needed lifting, and in Bert's experience a dance, some lively music and stew and bread would do just that!

Bert had already selected the next campsite. There was water and an easier place to guard.

Passing word to the outriders, Bert instructed them on setting up a lookout rota. The men knew what to do.

Then he rode down to the head of the train and, as each wagon went by, he passed on the news of the night's activities. Word soon spread and Bert could feel the excitement it generated.

His euphoria was dented, however, by the return of the riders he'd sent to look for Ardal.

'We scouted round, boss, but there was no sign of him. I figure he's followed the blood trail.'

Bert sighed. Removed his hat and wiped the inside with his bandana. He could only hope that Ardal ran into Arnie and the posse, and not into the clutches of the outlaws.

'Thanks, boys,' Bert said eventually. 'We'll set up camp in the next valley, I figure the lead wagon'll be there in four hours. Shouldn't take more than another two for the dust-eaters to arrive. You boys pass the word, OK?'

'Sure thing, boss.' The men rode on ahead.

Arnie and the posse had reached a point about 2 miles ahead of Ardal. Raising his hand, Arnie brought the riders to a halt as he checked the ground. The trail was narrow, almost like a mountain goat path, the land alternately soft soil and hard rock.

Hoof prints. Not that old either. Shoed horses, but he couldn't tell how many yet. More than one, he knew that.

'They came this way,' he said. 'Check your weapons, boys.'

Like all experienced cowboys, one cylinder was always kept empty in handguns. On many occasions, a fully loaded weapon had been known to fire off the round under the hammer, injuring rider or animal, so it was a good practice and quickly learned.

Now, everyone loaded in the extra slug into the empty chamber. Every shot would count.

Moving off slowly and of necessity in single file, the posse walked their horses higher up the pass. Arnie, leading, his senses acute, scanned the trail ahead, trying to figure out how many men they were up against.

The shot, when it came, sounded like thunder, as the explosive noise reverberated off the rock walls.

Arnie's horse reared too late.

The slug took Arnie high up in the chest, blasting him from the saddle. One foot came free of the stirrup but the other was caught fast in the other stirrup and his horse set off hell for leather, Arnie was dragged mercilessly across the rocky ground,

Had the slug not killed him outright, the rocks would have done. Within minutes, his clothes were shredded and gore was laid on the ground.

The remainder of the posse had reined in and stared in disbelief at the body of the man they had thought invincible as it was dragged in a macabre death dance along the trail. Momentarily, they were stunned. Unable to move, the second shot rang out and another rider was blasted from his saddle.

A clean kill, the man hit the ground, raising a huge plume of dust mixed with his own blood. His eyes were wide open with the look of surprise evident on his young face.

Wheeling their mounts on the narrow trail was not an easy task. Confusion and panic set in as the animals snorted and pranced, the whites of their eyes showing and their ears laid flat as the men dug their spurs in deep and yanked ineffectively on the leather reins.

A third shot rang out. The shooter was cool and

accurate. A third man, back-shot, slumped forwards in his saddle. The horse reared and whinnied, not knowing which way to turn as the third shot echoed its death rattle.

The fourth shot, the one that turned out to be more devastating for the surviving riders, rang out.

No man was hit, but a horse was hit in the neck, blood pouring from the wound.

The animal halted in shock, sagged, slipped and, as if in slow motion, fell to the ground, effectively blocking the trail and the only means of escape.

That fourth shot had been deliberate.

Now it was not only the animals that panicked.

Drawing weapons, the remaining six men began shooting wildly. They had no idea where the sniper was, only his general direction. But their handguns were uselessly out of range.

A fifth shot tore into the body of another man. The shot seemed to nearly sever his upper arm. He fell heavily on to the rocky trail and didn't move.

Harry was enjoying himself. This was easier than a turkey shoot. He made every shot count.

As he fired off his third shot, Clem and Marty joined him. Jed slept on.

'Hellfire, Harry, damn fine shootin'!' Clem said as he raised his own rifle to his shoulder, rested his left elbow on a rock, sighted down the long barrel and squeezed the trigger.

66

A smile creased his craggy features as he watched his target topple from his horse.

'You figure how many there are?' he asked Harry.

'Nope. Jus' figured I'd start a-shootin' 'em. Reckon there ain't as many left now,' he leered and spat.

Marty, not to be outdone, took aim with his own weapon and squeezed off another shot.

'Yeeha!' he whooped as another defenceless rider collapsed.

'Looks like they're high-tailin' it, or tryin' too,' Clem said.

'Shot me one o' their horses, they ain't ridin' out that easy!' Harry smirked and unleashed another deadly slug.

'They sure ain't gonna mess with us no more,' Marty grinned, showing blackened, tobacco-stained teeth.

One of the posse managed to escape the massacre. He sent his horse at a wild gallop down the narrow trail, head low, spurs digging in ruthlessly, and whipping his mount to urge more speed.

It was a dangerous and foolhardy move. The metal shoes of his horse found little purchase on the uneven ground and his fate seemed sealed when, losing control of its own legs, the animal belly-flopped.

The rider managed to stay atop as the horse struggled to his feet. Sweat- and foam-covered, the beast was now as afraid of his owner as he was of the shooting.

The near accident seemed to bring the rider to his senses. Although still panicked, he patted the animal's neck, muttering soothing words in the horse's ears. He urged the animal on, first a walk, then a gentle canter, keeping low in the saddle, offering as small a target as he could.

Sweat ran freely, the hairs on the back of his sun-reddened neck stood on end as he anticipated his own death at any moment.

He was lucky. It never came.

Missing the turn-off on the trail where the posse had bypassed the steep slope leading down to the burning wagon, he cantered on. No shots followed him and his breathing came easier as he pulled back on the reins, patting the horse's neck again in grateful thanks.

He'd survived.

Turning, he peered back along the trail, his ears straining for any sounds, his eyes watering with the strain of trying to catch any sign of movement.

No one was following, he was safe. He removed his sweat-stained Stetson and wiped the inner band with his bandana, replaced it, and walked his horse on.

'Hold it right there, mister.'

Ardal heard the shooting. He reined in and listened, trying to judge how far away they were. It was impossible, the rock walls made the sounds come from everywhere.

The gunfire stopped as suddenly as it had begun.

Straining every sense, Ardal waited. The silence was deafening and sweat began to form. He led his horse off the trail and ground-hitched it behind a craggy boulder.

Whatever had gone on ahead, Ardal was determined to play it safe. Was it the posse? Had they found the murderers? Who had won?

All these questions flitted through his mind. He also thought of Kate and the two children. He wasn't about to risk their future, or his, unless he knew what he was up against. He waited to see who, if anyone, appeared on the trail.

The time seemed to drag and the sweat seemed to build, although the temperature was quite low at this height. He knew his nerves were getting the better of him. He was a farmer, not a killer!

Having almost decided no one was coming towards him and about to holster his gun, he caught the faint sounds of hoofs.

He pulled back behind the boulder, ears straining. He was sure it was a lone rider, and not in any hurry either. Peering out, he looked up the trail and saw a lone horseman.

Pulling back behind the boulder, he waited, judging the best time to halt the man and find out what was going on.

'Whoa! Don't shoot mister!' the rider flung up both hands.

Ardal recognized the man, but from where? 'Keep those hands high,' Ardal repeated. 'Who are you?'

'Barton, Jess Barton, I work fer Mr Henman.' Ardal released the hammer of his gun and, after a moment's hesitation, holstered it.

'OK, tell me what's going on? What was all the shooting?'

'You ain't one of 'em, then?' Jess asked, still shaking and hands still above his head.

'Nope. Name's Ardal Maloney, my wife and children are on the train,' Ardal replied.

Slowly, Jess lowered his hands. 'Mind if I git down?'

'Sure, go ahead.'

'They ambushed us, Mr Maloney. We didn't stand no chance. We was cut down like dogs.'

'How come you got away?'

'I was at the back. There was a sharpshooter, we couldn't even see him, let alone return fire, an' the trail was narrow, we couldn't turn none too easy, and the shots jus' kept a-comin' and I watched men thrown from their horses an'. . . .'

'OK, OK, calm down, boy. How far up the trail was this?'

'No more'n a mile, two at the most. I was on my way to Mr Henman.'

'Well you better get back to him and raise the alarm. How many men were there?'

'Nine of us, couldn't say how many of them there was. We never saw a thing.'

'Stay calm and pass on the info to Bert. Tell him I'm going to shadow those murderin' scum. OK?'

'You can't miss where we got to,' Jess began, 'it was a massacre, a massacre!'

'I'll check 'em out, just in case there's any survivors,' Ardal assured the boy. 'Just make sure you get back to Bert, OK?'

Jess Barton nodded dumbly. He fumbled in his saddle-bags. 'Here, you better take these.' He handed over a box of bullets. 'There's fifty rounds in there, my pa gave 'em to me.'

'Thanks, Jess, 'preciate that. I'll make sure you get 'em back. Now get goin'.'

Jess mounted up. 'Take care, mister, them's no-goods up there.'

'I will, you jus' make sure you tell Bert everything that happened. By the way, how'd you get up here? You didn't come on the same trail as me,' Ardal said as the boy prepared to leave.

'Followed a trail to the north of here, I been looking for the tracks. Guess I missed 'em.'

'Well, the trail down yonder is steep, you'll have to walk your pony. Take care.'

Tipping his hat, Jess answered. 'Yes sir, Mr Maloney.

'It's Ardal, Jess.'

'Ardal.' Jess smiled and rode on.

'One of 'em got away, Clem,' Harry Manson turned to his boss.

'Yup, an' that spells trouble. Go check on Jed, see how fit he is. He ain't woken up yet.'

'OK, Clem.' Lazily, Harry stood and ambled down the rock face to their base camp.

'We get 'em all?' Marty said as Harry arrived.

'Nope, one got away.'

'Shit, you want me to go after him?'

'Wait till Clem gets down here. How's Jed?'

'Sleeping like a baby,' Marty said.

'You checked him out?'

'Nah, figured he's better off sleeping.'

'Hmm.' Harry crossed to the other side of the camp and knelt by Jed's sleeping body.

'Jed! Jed, wake up.' Harry roughly shook the sleeping man's shoulder.

'Wha'? Who, the hell?' Jed wiped his eyes.

'How ya feeling, *amigo*? We gotta vamoose pretty soon,' Harry said.

'Hell, how do I know? I jus' done woke up.' Harry lifted the blanket covering Jed's body and took a long look at his leg.

'Bleedin's stopped.' he said. 'Can you move your leg some?'

Sitting up slowly, Jed said: 'Had me a crazy dream, guns blasting all over the place.'

'That weren't no dream, *amigo*. The posse showed up, we got 'em all, 'cept one.'

'Hot damn! Why didn't ya wake me?'

'No time, buddy. Taken care of, but we gotta git going pretty damn soon. Think you can ride?'

'Sure. No problem. Jus' give me a hand up, a bit stiff is all.'

'You hang on there, no sense in moving till ya have to.'

'OK, cuppa coffee wouldn't go amiss,' Jed winked hopefully.

'OK, coming up,' Harry replied, and rose to his feet, satisfied that Jed was at least mobile.

Clem had arrived back at the campfire at the same time.

'No sign of any more riders,' he said. 'How's Jed?'

'He's OK, he'll be able to ride.'

'Good, then let's get movin'. They send a bigger posse and we're done for.'

Harry poured coffee in a tin mug and stood. 'OK, give me five minutes.'

'Make it four!' Clem said.

Harry smiled, but it wasn't a smile of amusement.

'You're going after him, ain't ya, Harry.'

'Can't let him raise the alarm. They got ten times the men we have an' I ain't about to die yet awhiles.

'You ride on, I'll catch you up. You know that.'

'No way I can make you change your mind?' Clem asked.

'You know me better'n that,' Harry said. He threw the dregs of the coffee on to the ground and mounted up.

Taking out the contents of one of the saddle-bags, he loaded his handgun and rifle.

Satisfied he was ready, Harry tipped his hat at Clem.

'*Adios, amigo.* Don't hang around and whatever you do, *don't* wait on me. That clear?'

'I guess, Harry. Good luck my friend and see you soon,' Clem said.

Ardal checked his weapons for the umpteenth time. How to go about this? I gotta make high ground, he thought. No point in putting my head in the same noose as the posse.

Nodding to himself, Ardal planned his moves. Right along the same trail, until he could see what remained of the posse, try and check the area out, leave his horse and gain some high ground, see if he could catch sight of where the outlaws were camped out. Then he'd have to play it by ear.

Mounting up, Ardal set his horse off at walking pace and he kept his pistol drawn. He didn't want any surprises along the trail.

Almost by accident, he found the ideal hiding spot for his horse; an almost enclosed small crevice in the rock. It was open to the air and covered in grass, there was even a small Cottonwood that seemed to be

74

growing out of the rock itself.

The entrance was just wide enough for horse and rider with barely inches to spare.

Ardal dismounted and removed his saddle and bridle, at least the horse would be comfortable. He then loosely ground-hitched the animal, making sure that, if attacked or spooked, his horse would be able to leave through the narrow entrance.

Taking his rifle and ammunition for both that and his handgun, Ardal left the crevice and began the long climb to the top of the trail.

Little did Ardal know that while he was settling his horse, Harry Mason had ridden down the trail searching for the missing posse member.

Jess was making good time. He felt relaxed now that he knew Ardal was guarding his back trail.

Jess should have used his head. The golden rule out in what was commonly called the Wild West, was never drop your guard and be aware all the time.

He could see the wagon train now across the prairie, it was no more than a mile away.

Behind him, Harry Mason was only 200 yards back and gaining quickly. Soon he would be in range.

Jess reined in to a gentle trot, his horse had done well that day and he didn't want to tire him out.

Harry, on the other hand, slowed to a gentle gallop and ate up the gap between himself and his quarry.

Harry pulled his rifle from the scabbard, reined in his horse and dismounted. He checked the scope and loaded the breech. Raising the rifle to his right shoulder, he sighted down the scope, making minor adjustments until he was satisfied.

There was no wind.

He placed his right index finger gently on the trigger, then held his breath as the man he had been chasing came into view and seemed so close Harry felt he could reach out and touch him.

Gently, as if he were caressing a woman, he started to ease the trigger towards him and, letting out his breath, he took another deep breath and held it.

Then he pulled the trigger.

Bert froze.

He waited for more shots, but none were heard.

'What the hell?' Bert almost shouted.

He scanned the terrain looking for – he didn't know what he was looking for. But someone had fired a rifle.

Then he saw the two horses and one man running to his mount.

'Get me my telescope.' Bert ordered. 'It's in my wagon. And hurry!'

By the time he got his telescope, the running man had mounted up and was riding hell for leather away from the wagon train.

'You want us to track him down, boss?' one the

outriders said.

'No, could be a trap,' Bert replied. 'I'll ride out and see who the other fella is. Keep your rifles handy!'

Keeping his rifle in his left hand, Bert mounted up and walked his horse towards the silent, and unmoving man, lying in the dirt.

As he neared the man, Bert suddenly recognized him.

'What the hell's happened, Jess?' Bert Henman took his Stetson off and started past Jess Barton, looking for the rest of the posse.

The trail was empty.

'They's all dead, Mr Henman.'

'Jeez! Arnie too? Dang near growed up with him!'

'Yes sir. I figure they're all dead.'

'*Figure*? Don't you know?' Bert was astonished.

Jess went on to tell the sequence of events to Bert. Although inside he felt guilty, Jess knew there was nothing he could have done to avert what had happened. If he'd tried to check all the bodies, he would surely have been killed, too.

Bert listened quietly, staring down at the ground. Jess wasn't sure, but he thought he saw tears in the old man's eyes.

'OK, son.' Bert took a deep breath and placed his hat back on his head.

'An' I ran into Mr Maloney, boss.'

'You what?

'Yes, sir, he figures on going after 'em. Tole me to

get back here and let you know.'

'Hellfire! I ain't got the men now to get back there!' Bert exploded.

'Maybe I could return,' Jess said, 'if'n you could spare, say, another two men?'

'You ain't in no condition to go anywhere 'cept the doc's house and get this bullet wound sorted. OK?'

'OK, boss,' Jess said and closed his eyes. In seconds he was asleep or unconscious.

CHAPTER SIX

The day was wearing on as Ardal slowly walked the trail. The hairs on the back of his neck were standing upright, every sound he heard could spell danger. Even his horse seemed to pick up on his unease.

Ardal kept his mind busy, alert, and concentrated: he felt danger all around him, and began to wonder if his move was wise.

Maybe he should get back to the train? he thought. The thoughts of Kate and Kevin and Patrick flitted through his mind.

Kate, he knew, would be worried sick. But she also knew he would take no unnecessary risks.

Like back in Ireland, when the English soldiers and landowners had forced the workers out of their homes, out of their jobs, to starve. Ardal had organized raiding parties to get much-needed food for their children. The danger had been just as terrible then, he'd seen what the soldiers did to those they caught.

He'd also seen the dead and dying children, lying by the roadside, waiting to be buried in mass, unmarked graves.

Ardal shook his head to rid himself of those images and concentrate on the job in hand. Ruthless killers.

Horses saddled, booty stashed, Marty helped Jed mount up, then mounted himself.

'We gonna stalk the train still?' he asked Clem.

Clem was silent for a few moments before, 'Hell, don't see no reason not to. Maybe we'll lie low fer a while, let 'em think we vamoosed.' A crooked grin split his face, but his eyes were icy cold.

'We done got rid o' their best riders, I reckon. Can't see 'em sending any more men out. Ol' Bert Henman ain't stupid. He'll be more concerned with the payin' folks that are alive, than the dead ones.' Clem laughed loudly.

'Bert Henman?' Harry looked puzzled.

'The trail boss,' Clem replied.

'You know him?' Harry asked.

'Sure, me'n Bert goes back a long way.' Again, Clem laughed. 'I killed his wife.'

The four men rode on up the trail.

'How's the leg feelin', Jed?' Harry asked his brother.

'Ain't too bad today, still sore some, but I'll manage,' Jed replied. But it was obvious the effort of mounting up and the jolting of his horse was causing him more pain that he wanted to let on.

'Figure we'll head higher, boys,' Clem said. 'Find us a place to stash what we already got, and then maybe hole up there a day or two. Speed that train's making, won't take us long to catch a look-see, maybe tomorrow, or the day after.'

The men nodded silently. Killers they might well be, hard, heartless men, but they weren't stupid. No point in trying anything on while the train was alert. Much better to catch them off guard.

Clem led the way out of the canyon, walking his horse steadily. There was no rush.

They reached the site of the massacre and Clem reined in.

'Harry,' Clem turned in his saddle. 'Git them weapons and ammo. Marty, you check them bodies over, see if'n they got any valuables or cash money on 'em.'

'Sure thing, Clem.'

Dismounting, the two men began their grisly search of the mangled bodies.

As if from nowhere, flies had already began their work too, and the men knew that pretty soon, after nightfall, the mountain critters would catch the scent of death.

High in the sky, buzzards circled, riding thermals,

biding their time before they felt it safe enough to land and rip the bodies to pieces in a frenzy of hunger lust.

'Plenty o' weapons and ammo, Clem,' Harry said, his arms full to busting with pistol belts and rifles.

'Ain't nothin' else here worth takin',' a disgruntled Marty called out, swatting flies as he spoke.

'Pity the horses bolted,' Harry said, 'we coulda done with a pack animal.'

'OK, let's git,' Clem said. 'We need to find a secure place to hole up, and no use in crying over spilt milk.'

Mounted again, the four killers rode on.

Bert Henman was in a dilemma: he badly wanted to send men back to help Ardal track down and kill the men who had ruthlessly murdered two families in his care. But having lost his chief scout and seven other men, it had left him short of hands and he had too many other people to look out for.

He sat atop his horse as the train slowly trundled past, then fate intervened. Kate was sitting on the next wagon. She turned her head and stared at Bert.

The message in her eyes was plain to see.

As she passed, her head turned slowly to keep Bert fixed with her eyes.

Bert knew then what he must do.

'OK, Jess. I'll allow two men to ride with you. But I'll pick 'em.'

'Sure thing boss,' Jess swallowed hard.

'I don't want no risk takin',' Bert added. 'You find Ardal, and you listen to him. What he decides to do, whether it's to track them scum down or ride back here, you follow! Got it?'

'Yes, sir.'

'OK. Go get me Bill and Rob.'

Jess wheeled his mount and rode to the head of the train. Within thirty minutes he returned with two outriders.

Bert Henman was staring into the sky, eastwards. 'Buzzards,' he muttered.

'Wanted us, boss?'

Bert turned to face the three men.

'Sure did, you just volunteered.'

'Fer what?'

Bert explained exactly what he wanted.

The two men didn't hesitate in their willingness to agree to go, especially when Bert mentioned a bonus!

'Go see Jack at the chuck wagon, grub up and get some ammo.'

The three men rode down the trail to find the chuck wagon, and Bert spurred his horse forwards to catch up to Kate's wagon and tell her what he'd decided.

He could see the expression on her face as she smiled, her gratitude obvious.

'I know Ardal will do what's best,' she said simply.

'I'm sure he will, ma'am. If'n there's anything you and the children need, you jus' see me, OK?'

'Thank you Mr Henman.'

'It's Bert, Mrs Maloney.'

'It's Kate, Bert,' Kate smiled.

'Kate,' Bert tipped his hat and set off to the front of the train.

The wagon train had made good time since the noon stop, albeit slow. There had been no hold-ups or accidents and Bert was beginning to think his luck had changed and that maybe, just maybe, they'd beat the snow in the mountains.

The sun was hanging low in the western sky, shadows were growing bigger by the minute and Bert knew he'd have to camp up soon. The trail was far too treacherous to risk so many wagons in the dark.

Bert reined in and awaited the return of his scouts. The early evening sky was clear to the west but, ominously, dark clouds were rolling in from the east. Taking off his gloves, Bert rolled a quirly and drew deep on the pungent smoke, the wind carrying the smoke away as it left his lips.

Turning to the sound of hoofs, Bert saw the first of the returning scouts. He listened patiently as the man gave his report of the trail ahead. The campsite was just over an hour away, again too small an area for a single circle up. In fact, they'd have to have three separate campsites, and that would take some manoeuvring.

'Picked up some sign, 'bout four, 5 miles yonder,' the scout said. 'Maybe twenty riders. The horses weren't shod, boss.'

'Shit! That's all we need! War party?' Bert asked.

'Cain't tell that, boss. Could be, could be renegades. Heard tell there was some hereabouts.'

'Better muster up some volunteers tonight,' Bert said, 'double the guard soon as we get camped out and stake out the cattle, that's what they'll be after.'

Bert thought for a moment.

'Single out a coupla steers and ground tie 'em on the trail,' he said eventually.

'You leaving an offering, boss?'

'If'n they're hungry, they'll take the steers and leave the wagon train alone, I figure,' Bert replied. 'It's worked well in the past.'

'An' if'n they ain't hungry?' one of the men asked.

'Well, if'n they ain't, we'll cross that bridge when we come to it. Now, let's get these good folk settled in.'

Slowly but surely, the wagon train ground to a halt. Three camps were formed in remarkably fast time, the would-be settlers now expert at manoeuvring their wagons.

Within thirty minutes, animals were tethered, fed and watered, kindling collected, campfires lit and water set to boil. Pretty soon, the alluring aroma of coffee and stew filled the air.

Word of Indians had spread quickly through the campsites; children were forbidden to leave the wagons, men armed themselves, and a sense of siege mentality pervaded. Every approaching horse was covered by as many as thirty rifles, and Bert hoped no one panicked and got itchy trigger fingers. He'd lost enough men already.

The children were fed first and despatched to their beds, with warnings of not to leave; men on first watch ate hurriedly, before taking up their positions on the perimeter, rifles checked and primed.

The women tidied up, washed dishes, kept the fires going and tended their children. The mood was one of defiance. These people hadn't journeyed this far to be thwarted by a band of renegades.

Bert dismounted at the chuck wagon, where Jack already had beans and bacon ready and a huge vat of coffee. Bert helped himself to the coffee and Jack dished up the food.

'Reckon they'll attack tonight, Bert?' Jack asked.

'Figure not. Injuns are superstitious people, they'll wait for sun-up no matter how hungry they are. They won't attack in the dark.' Bert sipped on the scalding-hot coffee and attacked the beans and bacon with relish. He hadn't realized how hungry he was!

'Staked two steers, yonder,' Bert said.

'Should keep 'em happy,' Red said.

'Well, we'll soon see,' Bert replied through a mouthful of beans.

Ardal Maloney reined his horse in and dismounted. No luxury of a fire and hot coffee for him. He unsaddled his animal and left the blanket on as he filled his hat with what little oats he had left and stroked the animal's nose as it fed hungrily.

He'd found a small cleft in the rocks, big enough for him and his horse. Sheltered from the elements, with a patch of tough rye grass, he looked up the rock face towering above him and saw the cleft narrowed chimney-style. There was no way anyone could get down there, so all Ardal had to worry about was the only way in – and out!

Unpacking his bed roll, Ardal went through his saddle-bags and, finding what was left of the jerky and a very stale biscuit, he settled down to eat.

There was a full moon and the ghostly blue-white light cast shadows that shimmered and moved as clouds scudded by high in the star-studded sky.

Ardal decided to risk a cigarette. He never smoked, and as the makings had been given to him, it seemed a good time to start.

Shielding the vesta, and averting his eyes to avoid losing night sight, he drew deeply and thought of Kate. She'd understand, he knew that, but he missed her and the children. Bert would keep an eye on them, of that he had no doubt, but he should be with them, not on this fool's errand.

Leaning back against his saddle, Ardal pulled the bed roll around him, made sure his horse was tethered securely and then closed his eyes.

It was going to be a long night.

Rob and Bill led the way along the trail the wagon train had taken earlier in the day. Dusk was falling and the two men smoked while Jess lagged behind them, all three sitting tall in their saddles.

They walked their animals at a leisurely pace, the ground too rocky and uneven to risk a lame horse: a man without a horse would die.

The wind was biting as they turned a bend in the trail, still climbing. The men hunkered in their trail-coats, pulled their Stetsons lower and leaned forward in the saddle. Even their animals lowered their heads as they walked directly into the bitter wind that seemed to turn their blood into ice and made their eyes water uncontrollably.

The three riders let their animals find the way, Jess figured they still had another hour before they reached the fork in the trail that led even higher into the mountains and the scene of the massacre.

For over thirty minutes the men trudged forward, fingers numb in leather gloves, faces freezing over and a chill running through their bodies as the merciless wind beat around them.

They rode single file, it was safer that way. To their right was a sheer drop into a seemingly bottomless chasm; it was too dark to see that far down. To their left, a rock wall that rose over 100ft and seemed to melt into the star-lit sky.

The trail narrowed and briefly turned out of the driving wind, then widened out again and the rock face to their left began to get lower. Scrub and the hardiest of vegetation appeared, their roots clinging on to whatever purchase they could find.

A small canyon opened up in the rock wall, big enough for the men to shelter, and with enough grazing for their horses. Wordlessly, the three men pulled rein and turned off the trail.

Muscle and bone stiff with cold, they dismounted, stamping their feet to get the circulation back, clapping gloved hands together as numb fingers began to throb as feeling started to return.

Instinctively, they tended their animals first, unsaddling but keeping the blankets on. The tough grass, though sparse, was enough for the horses to graze on.

'Should we risk a fire?' Jess asked, hopefully.

Rob was silent for a few moments but answered, 'Cain't see why not, what you think Bill?'

'Ain't likely them critters'll be heading thisaways, least, not fer a while.'

Jess searched for kindling and, finding a sheltered spot, began to build a campfire.

The wood was bone dry and he had no trouble lighting the fire, the wind fanning the flames. Coffee pot on, the men hunkered around the fire, warming cold limbs. Coffee boiling and beans and bacon in the pan, the three men began to warm, the inner man, too.

A shower of sparks flew into the air, lighting up their campsite briefly before being carried away on the cold mountain wind. It took the three men several seconds before they realized the glowing embers had shot skywards because an arrow had thudded into the fire.

Pulling their weapons out, the men took what cover there was and waited, ears and eyes straining to see or hear the slightest movement or sound.

There was nothing.

A second arrow whistled through the canyon, harmlessly striking rock.

'You see anything?' Rob whispered.

'Not a dang thing,' Bill replied.

'Well, there's only one way in,' Rob said.

'And out!' Bill added needlessly.

'Injuns attacking at night?' Jess said, his voice incredulous. 'I thought that never happened.'

'Well, it has now,' Rob said, keeping his eyes peeled as he scanned the area. 'Must be desperate.'

Bill loosed off a shot.

'There!' he said, 'I saw somethin'.'

Jes and Rob opened up, firing blindly. Their exploding weapons, the slugs ricochetting off the rock face and creating an almighty din that reverberated and echoed back and forth, making their ears ring.

90

They stopped firing.

The silence was now almost as deafening.

Nothing moved. They heard no sounds.

Bill grunted, and then slowly slumped. Both Jess and Rob heard the hiss of his breath. 'Bill?' Rob grated. 'Bill?'

There was no reply. Nor would there be.

The arrow had pierced Bill's neck. A fountain of blood pumped briefly, the jugular was severed. Rob crawled towards his partner. 'Jeez!'

Jess, on the other side of the narrow canyon, could see nothing.

'What? What's wrong?' he called out.

'Bill's dead!'

'Oh God,' Jess breathed.

'We gotta move back aways,' Rob said. 'It's too open here, they're gonna pick us off. On the count of three, Jess, move back. I'll cover you.'

Jess gulped, audibly.

'One . . . two . . . three!'

Taking a deep breath, Jess half rose. Keeping low, he scurried deeper into the canyon to the sound of Rob's firing.

'OK, Rob, there's cover a-plenty back here,' Jess called out.

'OK, Jess, keep your firin' to the left, your left. I'll make my way back on the right side. OK?'

'Sure, Rob, my left. OK, one . . . two . . . three!' Jess opened up with covering fire as Rob made his way back. Neither man could see much of anything, but Rob was aware of the whoosh as arrows flew past him and heard the metallic clunk as they clattered harmlessly against rock.

All except one arrow.

As Rob turned to one side to get behind cover, a searing hot pain shot up his right thigh. He slumped behind a boulder, gritting his teeth.

'I been hit, kid,' he said.

Jess left his cover and crawled over to Rob's side.

'Where ya hit?'

'Leg, high up in my thigh! Jeez,' a grunt from Rob.

Jess put his rifle on the ground and moved closer to Rob's side.

'That's gotta come out, Rob. You know that.'

'Sure, kid. Can you do it?'

Jess gulped. 'Sure,' he said, his voice more confident than he felt.

'You know what them pesky Injuns put on arrow heads?' Rob asked.

'I heard,' Jess swallowed.

'You got plenty of black powder?' Rob fought to keep his voice level.

'Yeah, I know what to do,' Jess replied.

'OK, let's do it, I'll keep watch for as long as I can. OK?' Rob stared hard into Jess's face.

Without saying a word, Jess grabbed a small piece of wood.

'You better clamp down on this, Rob,' he said.

'Do your best, kid,' Rob answered, and gripped the wood between his teeth.

Taking out his knife, Jess cut through the thick denim of Rob's pant's leg and opened up enough to get a clear view of the wound. He swallowed hard.

The arrow hadn't gone straight through, but was embedded deeply. To pull it out would cause even more damage as the barb would rip Rob's thigh to shreds. There was only one thing to do.

Hunkering down, Jess saw that the arrow head was not plumb centre, so maybe it had missed bone.

'I gotta push it through, Rob.'

Taking the wood out of his mouth Rob said, 'Figured that, kid.' He slowly replaced the wood and gripped it tight.

Putting one thick leather glove on his right hand, Jess gripped the arrow shaft in his left, and with his palm flat on the end of the shaft, he pushed with all his might.

Jess wiped beaded sweat from his forehead and took a deep breath.

Taking a slug from his gun-belt, he prised off the lead tip and carefully poured the black powder on both entrance and exit wounds.

He took out a vesta from his back pocket and, taking another deep breath, flicked the vesta on his thumbnail and ignited the black powder on the entrance wound.

The explosion, though small, was enough to make

Rob's leg jump involuntarily.

Then he did the same to the exit wound.

The stench of the exploding black powder coupled with the nauseatingly sweet smell of burnt flesh, made Jess gag a taste of bile in his mouth.

The deep, agonizing groan that escaped Rob's clenched jaw echoed round the canyon.

CHAPTER SEVEN

Ardal woke with a start.

Was it a dream? Had he heard gunfire? It took him several seconds to orientate himself fully.

Gunfire again. It was real, he hadn't dreamed it at all.

Throwing off his blanket, he stood and walked to the trail, gun drawn.

Two more shots were loosed off, then silence. Straining, Ardal tried to pinpoint at least the direction of the gunplay, but the mountains made the shots come from every direction.

Then he caught the briefest glimpse of something red in the sky, although vague and lasting only seconds, Ardal was sure it was sparks from a fire, and it was close. At least he now had a direction.

Running back to his horse, Ardal grabbed his rifle, his brain working overtime.

Was it the outlaws or another posse?

He had to find out.

Moving stealthily, Ardal moved back down the trail. There were no sounds now, and the eerie glow from the moon gave the scene a surreal atmosphere.

Keeping to the rock wall, Ardal made his way down the trail, rifle cocked and keeping one hand on the rock face, alternately checking his footing and peering ahead for any sign of movement.

Then he heard the snort of a horse.

Close.

It was another thirty minutes of silent walking before Ardal saw the horses. There were five of them, pintos and no saddles.

Indian horses.

Swallowing, Ardal stopped in his tracks. One man was guarding the animals, which meant four others were lurking nearby.

Inching closer, Ardal leaned his rifle against a rock and pulled out his Bowie knife, instantly remembering Kate's face when he showed it to her. It was the biggest knife she'd ever seen and had called it a sword. She said they were going to farm, not join the Three Musketeers!

In the pale moonlight, Ardal couldn't help but grin as the thoughts flitted through his head.

Taking a deep breath, and hoping the four missing Indians weren't too close, Ardal edged forwards. Whatever they were doing, they were up to no good.

Then he halted in his tracks.

What if they were attacking the outlaws? That was a possibility that hadn't occurred to him.

It would be ironic if he helped rescue the very people he'd set out to track down and . . . kill?

Kill! That was the first time he'd actually thought about what he would do if and when he caught up with the murderers.

He crept closer, knife held firmly in his right hand. He could see the faint glow of a campfire. Given the circumstances, Ardal thought, a pretty dumb idea to advertise your presence with a fire.

As he watched, another Indian appeared, bringing with him two horses: the sound of the horses' shoes telling Ardal they weren't Indian ponies.

Then he held his breath. He recognized one of the animals; he'd seen it recently.

Jess. The rider he'd sent back to alert Bert Henman!

Clear in his mind now as to what he had to do, Ardal kept watch as the second Indian handed over the reins of the two horses and went back into what Ardal could only assume was a small canyon, obviously bigger than the one he had camped in.

Then he remembered passing this spot. He'd passed it earlier in the day, just as night was falling, and decided the canyon was too big and exposed for safety.

So Jess *had* returned, and with a posse. But how

many men were in there? Surely Bert would send more than two men?

Straining with concentration, he listened for sounds of movement above the noises made by the animals.

Ardal's brain was in a turmoil. Should he kill the Indian tending the horses, or merely knock him out? Ardal had never killed a man, although he'd come pretty close back in Ireland, and couldn't help thinking, subconsciously, of whether the man had a wife and children, mother even.

Thinking of his own family, he made up his mind.

Creeping ever closer to the lone Indian, who seemed more intent on staring into the canyon than keeping a lookout, Ardal got to within 2ft of the man before he turned, as if some sixth sense had warned him.

Ardal, using the butt of the knife, caught the man on the side of the head and he fell like a limp rag. Going to Jess's horse, he searched for a rope. There wasn't one there.

Improvizing, Ardal removed the leather reins from one of the ponies and bound the prone figure. Then, removing his bandana, he wound it tightly across the man's mouth.

Man? Ardal thought, this was no more than a boy. Seventeen, if that. He was glad he'd made the right decision.

Lifting the body under the armpits, Ardal moved

it 10ft away from the horses, who hadn't batted an eyelid, and leaned him against a boulder near his rifle.

Grabbing the weapon, he then made his way back to the canyon entrance, where he halted, rifle in hand, and peered cautiously into the near impenetrable blackness.

It took a while for his eyes to adjust, then he saw the dim glow of the campfire and three saddles arranged around it.

So that was it? Three men?

He looked to either side of the campsite and saw the staring eyes. The man didn't move and the eyes didn't blink, the glow of the fire reflecting from them dimly.

So the Indians had killed one of the men.

As he watched, he saw a shadow half-stand and pull an arrow from a low-slung quiver. Then another shadow and another arrow was being loaded.

Ardal had to act, and act quickly!

Sighting down the long barrel of the rifle, Ardal loosed off a shot. He watched as the Indian slumped forward, arrow unfired.

The second man whirled round, bow taut, and Ardal had time to see the lethal barbed tip as it caught the dull glow of the campfire. He knew he couldn't draw and shoot in time and stepped backwards quickly behind the rock face just as the arrow scudded against rock, sparks flying, before it shot off harmlessly into the darkness.

A shot rang out. The second Indian, having exposed himself to shoot at Ardal, had been an easy target for Jess's handgun.

Ardal reloaded the rifle, then he removed his Stetson and placed it on the barrel of the weapon, slowly moving it out into view of whoever was in the canyon.

Nothing happened: no arrows or shots. Retracting the rifle, he donned his hat and gingerly stepped into the canyon.

Three down, two to go, he thought bitterly. But where in hell were the other two Indians?

'Jess? It's Ardal. Ardal Maloney,' he called out.

'Mr Ardal? Thank God!' Jess replied.

'You OK?' Ardal called again.

'I am, but Bill's dead, and Rob's in a bad way.'

Fingers of dull red light were beginning to escape the prison of the cloud cover, and Ardal was thankful for that at least. With the sun up, and light, would come a modicum of warmth. Easier to see, and be seen! He shivered involuntarily.

'I reckon there's two more of 'em yet,' Ardal called. 'Watch your back, I'm comin' in!'

'What the hell!' Clem Watkins sat bolt upright, his pistol already cocked and drawn.

'Huh?' A sleepy-eyed Harry Manson turned lazily under his bed roll.

'Shots, I heard shots,' Clem said, standing now and peering round.

'Didn't hear a dang thing,' Harry muttered.

Clem threw some more wood on the nearly dead campfire, sparks rising on the thermal of hot air.

'Wass goin' on?' Both Marty and Jed sat up slowly.

Harry, still under his blanket, muttered, 'Clem thought he heard some shots.'

'I didn't *think*, I *heard* 'em!' Clem insisted.

'Well, if there was any, an' I ain't sayin' there was, but if there was, they was far away, boss,' Marty said, and slumped back down under his blanket.

'It weren't *that* far,' Clem grumbled. 'Not far enough to be the wagon train, anyways!'

Harry eventually sat up at this. 'You reckon someone's trackin' us, Clem?

'Could be, could be. I don't aim to take no chances. Break camp, we're movin' on a-ways.'

Jed groaned. His leg was sore, and the thought of saddling up again filled him with dread. The pain seemed to be getting worse – not better!

'Coffee first?' Jed asked hopefully. 'If'n there was gunfire, then whoever it is has their hands full for a-whiles yet.'

Harry read between the lines and put the coffee pot on to boil.

Jed breathed a sigh of relief.

He would have preferred a good slug of whiskey, though.

101

The coffee time didn't last as long as Jed would have liked, but, with Harry's help, he managed to get atop his horse. The pain in his leg was excruciating, and he gritted his teeth, trying hard not to let it show.

He just hoped and prayed he stay in the saddle.

Dawn was breaking and already campfires were stoked up and water put on to boil.

The men on last watch returned to their families after a peaceful, if boring and long, night.

Jack at the chuck wagon had been up for over two hours already. Fresh biscuits cooked, beans and bacon were ready for the crew, and the giant coffee urn was bubbling away. The air was full of tantalizing aromas.

Breakfast was, for the crew, the best meal of the day as they rarely ate until nightfall. The scouts would be out and about, riding point and checking on the trail ahead for hazards, as well as guarding the flanks against intruders.

'No sign of Jess an' the boys?' Jack, the cook, asked Bert as the trail boss helped himself to a coffee.

'Nope, not yet. Reckon they won't catch up to him, if at all, till this mornin' anyway. They left pretty late in the afternoon.' Bert sipped on the scalding brew and smacked his lips together.

'How's the Irish lady an' her kids doin'?' Jack handed Bert a plateful of beans and bacon and a biscuit.

'She's doin' fine,' Bert said, sitting on a barrel and scooping beans into his mouth.

'An' the survivors of the bushwhacking?' Jack pressed.

Bert swallowed. 'They's doin' OK too, being well looked after.'

'Good,' Jack went back to serving the food to the queue of hungry cowboys, who waited patiently, tin plates in hand.

They never got to eat.

From one of the other wagon circles, gunfire erupted. And floating on the air came the war whoops of Indians.

Dropping plates and mugs, the men ran to their horses, mounted and rode hell for leather.

The third camp, slightly smaller than the other two, was located no more than a quarter of a mile away around a gentle bend, so it was almost isolated.

Bert led the way and within minutes they had the campsite in view. Already, three or four wagons were ablaze and more flaming arrows flew through the air. Bert reined his men in to assess the situation.

The Indians hadn't broken through the circle yet, and there were too few of them to circle the train, so they rode back and forth, gripping their ponies with their knees and loosing off arrows at a frenetic rate.

Out of shot, Bert saw two Indians. They were firing the flaming arrows.

103

'OK, here's the plan,' Bert said. 'You four,' he indicated four riders, 'take out those two Indians yonder. Split up and attack from both sides. Rest of you, follow me. We'll ride into the camp from the rear and add our gun power to those folks. Let's go!'

Bert and his men reached the camp and dismounted. Women and children were passing buckets of water from the small creek in an attempt to put out the blazing wagons, while up front, every able-bodied man was firing at the Indians, more womenfolk reloading their weapons to keep up a constant barrage.

'They ain't got no guns?' Bert asked the nearest man.

'No, Mr Henman, but they sure can fire them there bows.' He pointed back to the centre of the circle, where a gang of more women were busy tending the wounded. To one side of them, four bodies lay untended: two men, a woman and a child.

Bert deployed his men and the extra firepower began to have an effect. More to the point, the four riders who'd gone after the flaming bowmen had also reached their target. Circling behind the two Indians, the men had dismounted and back-shot the pair, so the danger of more fire was eliminated.

It took a further ten minutes before the attacking Indians were defeated, all except one brave. Driven by blood lust, the sole surviving Indian made a suicidal attack towards the wagon train.

Fortune seemed to favour him for a while as he galloped closer and closer, a maniacal scream coming from his throat and a tomahawk raised high in the air. Even his pony seemed possessed; ears flat against its head, eyes blazing, the whites showing, and a steady stream of foam dripping from its gaping mouth.

Bert had reloaded his rifle and, resting the long barrel on the footboard of a wagon, he took careful aim and squeezed the trigger.

The slug took the Indian dead centre in the chest. A fountain of blood erupted and the brave somersaulted backwards off the charging pony.

A dull thud filled the air as the body landed in the dirt.

The pony kept charging forwards for a few more yards before realizing it was riderless. In blind panic, the horse skidded to a halt inches from the wagons.

In the distance, the four riders were checking the bodies, making sure there'd be no surprises.

The flames were eventually doused and Bert was thankful that only four people had been killed. But there'd have to be a lot of reorganizing to make up for the lost wagons.

Three were burned out completely, meaning families had lost everything they possessed. Two more had lost canvas only, they could be repaired easily, but placing three families would be hard.

'What tribe?' Bert asked as his riders returned.

105

'Hell, boss, they seemed a mish-mash, some Cherokee, a Sioux, even an Arapahoe. I don't know what the hell's going on there.'

'Any survivors?' Bert asked.

'Nope. Neery a one. What you want us to do with the bodies, boss?'

'Hell I don't know. Cain't bury 'em out here, ain't enough places to dig. Cain't leave 'em there neither. Dammit! As if I ain't got enough to figure already.'

'Mebbe we can just cover 'em with rocks, least-ways it'll stop the critters getting at 'em.'

'OK, boys, see to it, I gotta see to the payin' folks and get them sorted. How many bodies were there by the way?' Bert asked.

'Counted fourteen, boss, mainly kids from what I could see. Ain't a one of 'em over twenty, I'd reckon.'

'What the hell's goin' on,' Bert said, 'the world's goin' crazy round my ears!'

Bert strode off to help in reorganizing the wagons. The four dead people were buried in the compound with all due ceremony. Wagons were repaired and families with room took on board those who'd lost their own wagons.

The wounded were tended, only time would tell if infection would set in. Most were leg and arm wounds, but one man had been hit in the chest and Bert didn't hold out much hope for his survival. His breathing was laboured and foamy blood gurgled from his lips, but he put on a brave face.

One look in his wife's eyes told another story. Bert left his men to help tidy up and get the wagons ready to roll. There was no time for sentiment when you were responsible for so many lives, and Bert figured he'd lost enough of these good folks and he didn't want to lose any more through the weather. So far they'd been lucky, the snows hadn't come yet, and Bert was hoping against hope they'd reach the plains before it did.

After a hurried breakfast, the well-organized routine of breaking camp was soon under way and Bert, now back at the main campsite, signalled Jack in the chuck wagon. Getting a thumbs up in return. Bert took his Stetson off and waved it aloft.

'Wagons, ho!'

Slowly, the first circle of wagons uncoiled, followed by the second and third and the wagon train was under way again.

Bert heaved a sigh of relief as he walked his horse alongside the chuck wagon. One more range to cross, he thought idly, staring at the mountains ahead. Just one more range.

Ardal slid to Jess's side, breathing heavily.

'How's your partner doin'?' Ardal asked as he looked at the still unconscious man.

'Well I took the arrow out, but I never got the chance to do anything else,' Jess replied.

'Well, you keep watch, I'll take care of it,' Ardal

107

said. He crawled to Rob's side and felt for a pulse. It was there, but faint.

Ardal took out his black powder and a box of vestas. He was glad the man was still out cold.

He could see that Jess had attempted to cauterize the wounds, but he hadn't used enough black powder. Blood, thick and dark, still oozed from both wounds.

Ardal had no choice but to do the job again.

Sprinkling the powder on both wounds, Ardal lit a vesta. He paused for a few seconds, then ignited the black powder.

The leg spasmed and a deep groan escaped the unconscious man's lips. But he didn't come to, he lay as still as the dead.

'Pass me your bandanna,' he told Jess. 'You got anything else?'

'Sure, I got a 'kerchief too,' Jess said as he handed both over.

Ardal inspected the wound; there was no bleeding and the blistered skin looked intact, at least for the time being. He had no experience of this at all.

He bound the wound, using the 'kerchief as wadding and securing it with the bandanna.

'Well, that's all I can do for now,' Ardal sighed. 'Just have to hope infection doesn't set in.'

Turning back to Jess, he asked: 'Any sign of those two pesky Indians?'

'Nope, not a sight nor sound,' Jess replied. 'They

sure are quiet.'

'Well, they're there someplace, just waiting for us to make a mistake I reckon. Keep low a moment,' Ardal said.

Using the same ploy as before, Ardal placed his Stetson on the rifle barrel and held it up.

The hat was aloft for no more than a couple of seconds when an arrow sliced through the hat rim.

'Jeez!' Ardal exclaimed, 'sure as hell glad I wasn't wearing that! But at least we got a direction now. Arrow came from our left and high up.'

Belly crawling, Jess edged forward slightly and scanned the rock face to their left.

The sun was rising rapidly, but to their left was in shadow. It would be noon before the whole canyon was light. They couldn't afford to wait that long. Rob had to be taken back as Ardal was sure he needed more help than he could supply and there was bound to be someone there who could doctor.

Uppermost in his mind also was the thought of losing track of the murdering scum he was after.

'It's impossible to see anything,' Jess said and pulled himself back in behind the boulder.

'OK, then on the count of three, take another look, I'll hang the old Stetson out to air again,' Ardal placed the hat on the rifle again. 'OK, one . . . two . . . three!'

Ardal slowly raised the rifle and Jess slid out again.

The *whoosh* of the arrow missed the hat this time

and clattered noisily against rock, the shaft shattering on impact.

'Got one!' Jess whispered as he came back in. 'Just caught a glimpse but I reckon I can get him if'n we do it again.'

'Well, third time lucky!' Ardal grinned.

CHAPTER EIGHT

Clem led his gang higher up into the mountains.

The path was steep, but the footing was good, so the horses, at a steady pace, made good progress.

Jed's leg was not getting any better. He knew, instinctively, that something was wrong. His worst fear was poisoning. He was hot, sweating like a pig and cold! The pain in his leg was excruciating and no matter how he sat, he couldn't ease the pain.

Clem seemed oblivious to Jed's agony, but Harry was keeping a close eye on his brother, although there was precious little he could do to help.

As they rounded a bend in the trail, a valley opened up to their left. Below them, they could see the long snake-like wagon train as it wended its way down. Clem knew that it would stop soon and camp up for the night. He halted and sat staring down at the wealth he meant to take. Nothing else mattered to him; money, or goods he could sell to raise money, was all that counted in his life.

When you got money, you can live the high life till it runs out; and when it runs out, you go get some more.

Their stash had been carefully hidden near their last campsite, ready to be collected when they'd finished.

San Francisco. That's where Clem wanted to be. Fine women, fine cigars, whiskey and the best room in the house, were the only thoughts he had on his mind. To hell with the rest of the boys, he thought, they didn't have his style. Maybe he should start looking for a gang that more suited his lifestyle?

As if in slow motion, Jed slid from his saddle and landed heavily on the hard-packed dirt. Harry was just too late to try and catch him.

'What the hell,' Clem turned angrily.

Harry dismounted and went to his brother's side. Felt for a pulse and breathed a sigh of relief when he found one.

'He's out cold, Clem,' Harry called up. 'We gotta camp up, he cain't go no further.'

'Hell! We ain't nowhere's far enough away yet!' Clem spat.

'Far enough or not, he cain't go on!' Harry was adamant.

Clem drew his sidearm.

'Maybe he needs putting outta his misery,' he drawled.

Harry stood slowly, his right hand resting on the butt of his own gun.

Clem cocked the revolver, menacingly.

'You better shoot me first,' Harry said between clenched teeth, cos I ain't about to let you kill my brother!'

Clem hesitated. Even though his weapon was drawn and cocked, he knew how fast Harry was and no way did he want to risk being shot way up here in the middle of nowhere.

Raising the barrel of his gun skywards, Clem released the hammer slowly and reholstered.

'Hell, I was only funnin' ya,' Clem said, a smile on his lips that didn't reach his eyes.

Harry's hand still rested on the butt of his handgun, but he relaxed. He knew he'd have to keep an eye out for Clem from here on in.

'I'll find a campsite and we can hunker down there fer a while,' Marty said to ease the tension in the air.

Kicking his mount's flanks he edged his horse forward.

Harry bent to attend his brother as Clem dismounted.

'He got the poisoning?' Clem asked.

'Reckon so,' Harry said. 'You got any o' that whiskey left?'

'Sure, I'll fetch it.' Clem walked back to his horse and rummaged through his saddle-bags, took out the bottle, removed the cork and took a slug before returning to Harry. 'Here, help yerself.'

Harry removed the bandanna from around Jed's leg to expose the wound. He reeled back as the stench hit him.

'Shit!' he said and stood up.

'He got the gangrene?' Clem asked.

Harry was still gagging as he nodded. 'What the hell do we do about it?'

'Seed it once down in Mexico,' Clem said lighting a quirly. 'Fella had it in his arm. Had to, er, amptate?'

'*Amputate!*' Harry said. 'Cut it off?'

'Yep, that's the word, amptate. Fella died anyways, jus' took him a whiles longer, is all.'

'Hell, I cain't cut Jed's leg off!' Harry said, a look of horror on his face.

'Well, if'n you don't he's a gonna anyways,' Clem said disinterestedly.

'I found a site,' Marty called. He looked at the two men standing by Jed. 'What's up?'

'Gangrene, I think,' Harry said. 'Clem reckons all we can do is cut the leg off.'

Marty dismounted and took a good long look at Jed's wound. 'Maybe not,' he said.

Harry looked at him. 'You done doctoring?'

'Hell, no! But I once seed a fella have skin cut away from a wound, and plenty o' whiskey poured over it. Next he poured black powder on it, still smell that burning. Anyways, the man healed up real good.'

Harry thought about that. Eventually, mind made up, he said, 'Then I'm gonna try that.'

'How far is this campsite, Marty?' Clem said, more interested in getting coffee brewing than anything else.

'Just ahead, a small blind canyon, an' there's water there too,' Marty replied.

'Can you take the horses, Clem, while me an' Marty bring up Jed?' Harry looked towards Clem, who was still quietly smoking.

'Sure thing, Harry.'

Marty led the three animals towards Clem. 'Up yonder, 100 yards or so, ya cain't miss it.'

Clem grabbed hold of the reins and walked his horse up the pathway, the other three horses trailing docilely behind him.

Grabbing an arm each, Harry and Marty placed Jed's arms round their shoulders and lifted the still unconscious man to his feet.

'Let's get this done,' Harry said, and the two set off at a slow pace to catch up with Clem.

'You ready, Jess?'

'Ready as I'll ever be!'

Slowly, Ardal raised the barrel of his rifle above the boulder, showing his battered Stetson.

They waited.

Nothing happened.

He moved it to one side and stopped.

115

Still nothing happened.

'Darn it, the redskin's cottoned on,' Ardal said.

'Or he's out of arrows,' Jess whispered.

'I doubt that, Jess.'

'You reckon they've gone?'

'Nope. Them bucks is out for glory. Either they're renegades or they're a hunting party, out to prove their bravery. I can't see 'em giving that up easy.'

'So what do we do now?' Jess asked.

'Well, we can't make a run for it, not with Rob the way he is, so we'll have to wait and see what their next move is.'

Ardal lowered the rifle and placed his Stetson back on his head, both men keeping a wary eye on the far rock face, making sure they didn't present an easy target.

'Better reload,' Ardal said, 'we need all the fire-power we can muster. And keep your head down, don't give 'em something to shoot at!'

Jess grinned, despite their predicament, 'I sure don'e aim to. . . .'

Jess never got to finish the sentence. The look on his face warned Ardal before Jess could utter a warning.

The two men were concentrating so hard on their quarry up on the rock shelf that they committed the cardinal sin of not keeping a watch on their backs.

Before Ardal could react, he felt a weight on his back, followed by a war whoop! He was flung flat on his belly, and all the air seemed to be sucked out of his lungs.

Jess could only stare at the Indian straddling Ardal's back, war paint adorning the man's face and body, his torso gleaming in sweat. Jess's eyes slowly moved up the man's powerfully muscled raised arm and saw the tomahawk raised, ready to deal a death blow.

Suddenly, Jess was galvanized into action. In the confined space, he found it difficult to manoeuvre the rifle round, clanging the barrel on rock in his panic to loose off a shot.

Time seemed to stand still as he brought the weapon up and squeezed on the trigger. He could even see the man's arm descending towards Ardal's head, with Ardal powerless to avert the death blow.

The slug caught the Indian across his chest, leaving a red score before burying itself in the upraised arm holding the tomahawk. Without making a sound, the Indian's grip on his weapon slackened, and the tomahawk clattered to the dirt. The man's right arm hung uselessly at his side.

Ardal twisted violently and made a grab for the tomahawk. At the same time, he managed to shuck the man off his back and against the rock to their rear.

Jess watched as if mesmerized as Ardal regained his feet and threw himself at the injured Indian. Ardal caught a glancing blow with the tomahawk on

117

the man's chest and this time a guttural grunt escaped the Indian's lips. Ardal raised the tomahawk to deal a death blow, but hesitated.

He couldn't kill a defenceless man.

He dropped the tomahawk and using his fists, pummelled the man into unconsciousness. As Ardal suspected, the Indian didn't have the strength to fight back.

Ardal stood and looked at the prone form of the man who'd tried to kill him, and a shiver went up his spine as the thought of being scalped filled his mind.

The Indian, although big, was still a boy, Ardal thought, no more than seventeen or eighteen.

Ardal sighed, wondering why the hell couldn't people learn to live together?

He didn't have time to dwell on that thought.

Jess turned in time to see the other redskin running towards him, also with a raised tomahawk. The man's eyes were wild and his mouth wide open as he yelled a blood-curdling scream.

He was now less than 30ft away and closing rapidly. Jess swallowed, he had no loaded weapon and the Indian looked well-muscled, large. Too large. It seemed Jess was able to take in every detail of the man. Long black hair, loose and flying out behind him. Brown eyes that stared straight at Jess, two white bands of war paint on each cheek of the man's face, bulging muscles.

And above all, Jess could see the stone tomahawk

raised above his head, ready to strike death.

Jess knew he wouldn't stand a chance in hand-to-hand combat. He brought the now empty rifle round just as the Indian flung himself towards Jess. The rifle barrel caught him in the stomach and, such was the force of the warrior's headlong rush, it penetrated skin, skewering the man in mid-flight.

Ardal stared, open-mouthed, unable to comprehend what had just happened, and powerless to help.

The wild-looking eyes changed to one of shock, the blood-curdling scream reduced to a grunt and groan as he landed on top of Jess.

Dead.

There was utter silence.

Jess scrambled out from beneath the giant body, his shirt covered in blood.

Ardal rushed forward, 'You hurt, Jess?'

'I don't think so,' Jess replied, feeling his body, too numb to know.

'Get that shirt off, let's see,' Ardal ordered.

Jess removed his blood-stained shirt to reveal a skinny chest, but above all, not a wounded chest.

'Guess it's all his blood,' Ardal said. 'You're clean.'

'That all of 'em?' Jess asked, his voice trembling, as was the rest of him.

'Reckon so,' Ardal replied.

There was a groan.

Both men froze.

'What was that?' Jess said.

'Shush!'

The groan came again.

'Maybe that Injun's coming to,' Ardal said. He picked up his rifle and turned towards the stricken man still leaning against the rock wall.

'Nope, it ain't him.' Ardal stood still, ears straining. 'Jeez! It's Rob!'

In the heat of the Indian attack, both men had temporarily forgotten about their wounded pard.

'Jess, you tie this Indian fella up, good and tight. I'll check Rob out. OK?'

'Sure thing,' Jess replied. He was a little relieved to be doing something.

Ardal walked back to where they'd left Rob after removing the arrow head.

'Rob, Rob? You OK?'

Rob merely groaned and shifted his weight.

'We gotta get him back to the train,' Ardal said. 'We can't wait for him to recover, and we can't take him with us!'

'What do you suggest?' Jess asked. 'Give up the hunt?'

'Nope. I reckon we use the Indian ponies and you take Rob back. I'll go on. If you can make it back, all well and good, if not. . . .'

The four outlaws reached the chosen campsite and dismounted, Harry helping Jed, who almost toppled from his horse.

Jed was bathed in sweat and well on the way to being delirious. He had no idea where he was, who he was with or what had happened. The pain in his leg was so bad he could feel nothing else.

Harry half-carried, half-dragged his brother to a comfortable spot, laid him down gently, and went for his bed roll.

Clem looked on dispassionately.

Getting his canteen, Harry tore off his bandanna and soaked it, then began mopping his brother's brow.

'Don't look so good, does he,' Clem said rolling a cigarette.

'He'll be OK once this fever breaks,' Harry said.

'You looked at his leg? I can smell it from here!' Clem spat and lit up his smoke.

'Just about to,' Harry replied. 'Hell, I jus' hope I can manage to git rid of it all.'

'Well, I only got two bottles left,' Clem added. 'An' one o' them's half-empty.'

Harry ignored the remark. By this time, Jed was beginning to rant and thrash around on the ground. Harry lifted his head, placed the whiskey bottle on his lips and started to pour.

Jed coughed and spluttered to begin with, but soon started taking gulps of the fiery and potent brew.

A quarter of the bottle later, his thrashing had stopped and his eyes rolled as the whiskey took effect.

Marty had built a fire, much to Clem's objection, but they needed to sterilize the knife, no point in introducing more germs.

'How's the blade doin'? Harry asked.

'Give it a coupla more minutes yet, Harry.' Marty thrust the blade deeper into the flames. 'It ain't red yet.'

'We better hold him down good and tight,' Marty said. 'I'll keep his legs still.'

'Clem, would you sit on his chest?' Harry asked.

'What ya doin', fellas?' Jed croaked as Clem lowered himself, not too gently, on Jed's chest.

'Hey, ya big galoot, get offa me!' Jed began to struggle, the panic in his voice evident.

'Just keep still, Jed,' Harry soothed, 'we gotta do this.'

'You gonna kill me? You are ain't ya, you're gonna kill me!'

'No, Jed, we ain't gonna kill you,' Harry replied, keeping his voice even.

With Clem straddling Jed's chest and Marty hanging on to his legs, Harry exposed the wound in Jed's leg.

The stench almost made the men gag.

With the wound open, Harry stared at what was just a small hole, but the hole was surrounded by black, dead skin and edged in a fiery red. Pus oozed from the hole. Turning his head away to take a deep breath, Harry took a swig from the whiskey bottle before pouring a liberal amount on to the leg.

Reaching for the red-hot blade, Harry began his gruesome task.

The scream that reverberated around the small enclosed area made the hairs on the backs of the men's necks stand up.

The scream was cut short and Harry thought Jed had passed out, but he couldn't see Clem's huge paw covering both the mouth and nose of his brother.

Acting quickly now before he lost his nerve, Harry cut deep into the flesh surrounding the wound, what was a small hole of perhaps half an inch in diameter soon became a gaping open sore three inches across. The stench got even worse, if that were possible, and it was all Harry could do not to throw up.

Gradually, the dead and blackened skin was removed. In the half-light, Harry peered into the open mess, searching for signs of gangrene.

'Maybe got into his blood,' Clem said, 'poison a man's insides.'

Clem kept his back to Harry and Marty, his hand still pressed hard against Jed's face. He could feel no movement in the man's chest and, certain he had rid himself of a problem, he slowly removed his hand and Clem rose.

'He's out cold now, no sense in me a-sittin' on him.' Clem grabbed the unopened bottle of whiskey and, pulling the cork out with his teeth, took a mighty slug.

Meanwhile, Harry, as sure as he could be that he'd cut enough flesh away, reached for the black powder.

'Give me a swig o' that,' Harry said before he poured whiskey into the open wound. Even unconscious, a groan escaped Jed's lips. Clem almost choked on his cigarette, how can a dead man groan?

The answer was simple: Jed *wasn't* dead!

Harry sprinkled the powder on to the wound. He raised the whiskey bottle to his lips, saying: 'I'm gonna need this!'

He handed the bottle back to Clem, who took another mighty gulp of the cheap whiskey before wiping his mouth and beginning to roll another cigarette.

Harry took a mouthful of the rotgut, passed the bottle to Marty and then poured more black powder on to Jed's leg.

'Here,' Clem said, and passed Harry a vesta. Taking a deep breath, Harry struck the vesta with his thumb and set the powder alight.

Jed's body convulsed as the small explosion lit the campsite.

Clem almost dropped his cigarette.

The sweet and sickly smell of burning flesh filled their nostrils and Marty, no longer able to hold it back, threw up on the ground.

Jed's body didn't move again.

Clem knelt down and felt the man's neck.

A grim smile spread on his lips, which he hastily hid.

124

'Ain't no pulse here, Harry,' he said, and removed his hat in mock respect.

Harry laid an ear on Jed's chest, but could hear nothing. He felt Jed's neck.

Nothing.

Behind him Clem's gruesome grin reappeared and, unbeknown to him, Marty saw it.

CHAPTER NINE

Bert Henman was in a quandary. His years of experience as a wagon train boss told him exactly what he had to do: keep the folks who had put their faith, trust and hope in him safe – above all else.

His heart told him otherwise.

The train trundled slowly down a small incline, the way ahead was clear and the Plains only two days, maybe three, ahead.

Hell, he'd beat the first winter snows yet, he thought.

All that filled his head now, though, was Ardal and whether Jess, Rob and Bill had made it to him and, more importantly, that Ardal was still alive!

Slowly, he made his way down the slope to re-join the wagon train as Red's chuck wagon drew alongside him.

Bert raised the brim of his Stetson a tad, rubbed a sleeve across his forehead and squinted back at the mountain range, almost willing his men to return, with or without the murdering scumbags. It was Red who broke into his reverie.

'Got a bottle in back if'n it helps,' Red said.

'Thanks, Red, but I need a clear head right now.'

'No word then?'

'Nope.'

Red paused for a moment, then lightly flicked the reins, rolling on.

Slowly, Bert rode back, howdying folks as they passed by, a false grin cracking his ruddy features as he tried his darnedest not to show his own personal fears.

Kate's wagon was approaching, and already he could feel her eyes burning into him, a host of unasked questions framed her face.

He brought his eyes up to hers and smiled.

She smiled right back, and nodded her head slightly. She understood.

Wordlessly, Bert tipped the front of his Stetson as she passed, and Kate turned her attention to the trail ahead.

Between them, Ardal and Jess managed to fashion a travois and attach it to one of the Indian's ponies. As carefully as they could, they laid Rob down on it and covered him in a bed roll, his fate now in the lap of the gods.

'You should be OK, Jess,' Ardal said. 'Just make

127

sure you stick to the trail. I reckon the path will be clear.'

'I don't feel good about this, Ardal,' Jess replied.

'It's what we gotta do, Jess. I'll be OK, I ain't about to risk my life any more'n I have to. But I cain't allow these murderin' scumbags to get away scot-free.'

'I'll get back as soon as I can,' Jess said, mounting up. 'Maybe I can bring more help.'

'Don't bank on it, Jess,' Ardal, said, smiling a smile that was forced. 'There's a lot of folks back there on the wagon train relying on Bert.'

'I hate to break in here,' Rob said, pain written all over his face, 'but I sure would like to git movin'!'

'Hell, sorry, Rob.'

Ardal watched as Jess, leading the Indian pony towing the travois, made his way slowly along the trail before disappearing around a bend.

Alone again, Ardal began to pack his meagre possessions. Then he heard a grunt.

His Colt appeared in his hand in a flash as Ardal spun round, his eyes seeking the source of the sound.

A grunt again.

The Indian! What the hell was he going to do with his captive?

Holstering his gun, Ardal stood and thought. He wouldn't – couldn't – kill the man in cold blood, enemy or not.

The Indian was still trussed and the gag in place as Ardal walked back behind the rock that had saved their skin.

Conscious now, Ardal stared back into the darkest brown eyes he'd ever seen. There was no fear there, nothing, just the blank stare of a man who thought he was about to die.

Ardal knew otherwise.

'What am I gonna do about you?' he said out loud.

The Indian blinked, a puzzled look on his face.

Ardal knelt and untied the bandanna from around his mouth, then, walking to his horse, grabbed the canteen, uncorked it, and poured a trickle of water into the man's mouth.

The man's eyes were still puzzled as he gratefully accepted the water.

'I ain't about to kill you, friend,' Ardal said softly, 'but I sure as hell can't let you loose yet awhiles, and I can't take you with me.'

'You hunt bad white men?'

Ardal stood. An amazed look on his face. 'You speak English?'

The Indian nodded. 'Small piece.'

'Then you know I ain't gonna kill you.'

The Indian nodded again.

'You killed my brothers.'

'Had no choice, *you* attacked *us*! We had to defend ourselves.'

The Indian sat silently for a while. Then he raised his head and spoke.

'My people are starving. The bluebellies drove us

from our homeland; the white men kill the buffalo, we have nothing to eat and nowhere to live. My father, our chief, went to the highest mountains and sat down to die. I will not do that!'

'I'm sorry, young fella,' was all Ardal could think of to say.

'If we don't fight, we die,' the Indian said.

'We gotta learn to live in peace,' Ardal argued.

'We signed a treaty with your president, it meant nothing when they discovered the yellow metal. We were driven off. The land we were sent to was barren, our children and the old died first in the cold winter. Now there are only a few of us left.'

'Maybe I can persuade the wagon train boss to separate out a few head of cattle, at least you'd get fresh meat,' Ardal said.

'You would do that?'

'I'd rather you were my friend than my enemy.'

'I know where the men you hunt are,' the Indian said.

That stopped Ardal in his tracks. 'You would tell me?'

'I would take you.'

'Why would you do that? It's ain't your fight.'

'You will try to feed my people, I will help protect yours. I am a man of honour.'

It took Ardal five seconds to make his mind up. Kneeling, he untied the leather thongs binding the man, then stood back as the Indian rubbed his wrists and ankles.

The man stood. 'I am Weeping Bear,' he said.

'Ardal, Ardal Mahoney,' Ardal offered his hand.

Unsure, Weeping Bear took it, they stared hard into one another's eyes, hands gripped tight and an understanding passed between them.

Releasing hands, Ardal stepped back. 'I got some sour belly and beans, and we better bind up that wound, too.'

'It's nothing,' Weeping Bear dismissed the wound as if it was nothing.

'The bullet in your arm?' Ardal asked.

'No, just flesh wound.'.

'Well, let's get a fire going, OK?'

With a word, Weeping Bear began to collect kindling, with minutes he had a small campfire going, while Ardal brought the food from the saddle-bags.

Fifteen minutes later, both men having soaked up the grease with stale bread, they had finished.

'You got many braves with you?' Ardal was uneasy.

'Three more, that is all. We were hoping to steal cattle from the wagon train, but the men you hunt have prevented that.'

'How so?' Ardal asked.

'Too many on guard,' Weeping Bear answered. 'No one seems to sleep.'

Ardal's eye caught sight of the tomahawk that had nearly ended his life. He walked over to it and picked it up. Weighing it in his hand, he looked at Weeping

131

Bear and, handle forward, handed it over.

Gratefully, Weeping Bear accepted it and tucked it into his belt. 'Thank you, my friend, it was my father's,' was all he said.

Silently, they packed the gear away, doused the fire and, while Weeping Bear collected his bow and arrows, Ardal brought his horse and Weeping Bear's pony.

'I'm afraid we used one of your ponies. Rob, one my helpers, was badly injured, so Jess has taken him back to the train.'

'I understand,' Weeping Bear said as he mounted up. 'We go to my camp, then we get your enemies.'

It was nearly an hour later that Jess caught sight of the wagon train.

'Nearly there, Rob,' Jess called over his shoulder.

There was no reply.

Reining in, Jess dismounted and walked back to the travois.

Rob was white, a whiter than white that seemed to make the blood redder. Kneeling, Jess felt Rob's neck. There was a pulse, faint, but a pulse.

Jess made up his mind: it would be quicker, and maybe safer, to leave Rob here and go get help.

Unstrapping the travois, he gently laid it on the ground, tethered the Indian pony and remounted.

Free of a trail horse, Jess kicked his mount into a gallop and headed down towards the wagon train.

Heedless of his own safety, Jess pushed his mare to the limit.

Scouts had seen the reckless rider long before Jess was aware of their presence.

Guns drawn, beads sighted, trigger fingers itchy, they waited.

Two hundred yards away now, Jess took his Stetson off and waved it in the air, yelping loudly at the same time to attract attention.

Hammers were eased back as rifles were lowered.

Bert Henman called a halt to the train and trotted his black stallion back along the line towards the advancing rider. A rider he recognized.

'Hold your fire, men. It's Jess!'

'Mr Henman, Mr Henman!' Jess yelled at the top of his voice, his horse still galloping wildly past astonished travellers.

Skidding to a halt and almost losing saddle, Jess reined up.

'We were attacked by Injuns! Mr Mahoney is OK, but they got Bill, and Rob is sore ill. I got him on a travois yonder, Mr Henman.'

'Whoa! Slow down, boy, now start at the beginning.' Henman dismounted and beckoned Jess to do the same.

'Red,' Henman called out. 'Get some men and bring Rob in. See what you can do for him.'

'Sure thing, boss.'

Jess then proceeded to bring Bert Henman up to

date with what had happened up in the mountains.

'So you killed one and one got away, and one you got tied up?'

'Yessir, Mr Henman, sir.'

'OK, boy, get yourself some vittles and a fresh mount, be ready to leave in fifteen minutes.'

Jess did all but salute as he tied the horse to the chuck wagon.

In the meantime, Red had returned driving a flatbed with Rob, carefully tended by two of the womenfolk.

'He'll live,' Red said to Bert. 'Take awhiles, but he'll be OK.'

'Get me two men willing to ride, Red,' Bert ordered. 'We're leaving in ten minutes.'

With fresh mounts saddled, food for two days and ammo aplenty, the four riders set off, Jess leading the way.

Harry Manson had wrapped his dead brother in a tarpaulin and tied the ropes good and tight.

Marty had helped dig the hole and found and piled up some loose rocks. Between them they manhandled the body and lowered it down. Because of the terrain, the hole was only 3ft deep and just wide enough.

Silently, the two men covered the body, Clem Watkins merely a bystander, watching the two men.

Occasionally, Marty threw him a glance, watching

134

the man's face. He was in a dilemma: should he tell Harry what he saw? Tell him what he thought? He was torn. One thing he did know: he could never trust Clem Watkins.

Piling the rocks tightly over the grave, Harry and Marty stood a while, head bent. Neither man said anything, each in their own thoughts. Harry, the loss of a brother; Marty knowing Clem had killed him.

'Come have a drink, boys,' Clem called out jovially, holding up a whiskey bottle and breaking the sombre mood. 'Digging's thirsty work I find.'

'You must be parched, then,' Marty said sarcastically.

'Now, now, Marty, too many cooks an' all that,' Watkins broke into a belly laugh.

'Glad you can find something to laugh about,' Harry said. 'I don't want a drink.' Harry walked to the perimeter of the campsite, sat down on a rock and rolled a cigarette.

Marty also ignored the offer of a drink. He'd made up his mind. Following Harry, he took out his own makings and sat beside him. Clem watched the two men intently; he was sure neither of them had seen him, but he was wily and prepared for anything.

Lifting the bottle to his lips, he took a swig of the liquor, feeling its warmth as he swallowed. A grin split his face as he watched the two silent men.

Marty drew deep on his cigarette, seeming to take courage from it. 'Harry, there's something I gotta say.'

135

'Spit it out, Marty.'

'OK, but don't look round or nuthin', OK?'

'Yeah, OK.'

'I don't think Jed died.'

'What? You crazy fool, we just buried him, didn't we?'

'No, I don't mean that, I mean, well, I think he was helped.'

'Waddya mean, "helped"?'

'Fer Chris'sakes, keep your voice down!'

'Spit it out, Marty,' Harry drawled impatiently.

'I saw the look on Clem's face when Jed died. He was smilin'! I don't think Clem wanted Jed to survive. Be too much of a burden. Now there's only the three of us to share the loot.'

Harry jumped to his feet. 'What was that?'

'What? I didn't hear nuthin'!'

'Shh!' Harry was staring down the canyon, his eyes flickering from side to side.

Clem slowly placed the cork back in the bottle and leaned it against his bed roll. At the same time, he picked up the Winchester that was never far from his side.

'Back here,' he called softly, 'slow and easy like.'

Pistols drawn, and all thought of the previous conversation forgotten – for now – Harry and Marty slowly backed up towards Clem.

'You hear any more?' Clem asked.

'Nope, but I sure as hell heard something out there!'

'Marty, get to that ridge up yonder, slow an' easy like. Harry, take the opposite side, anyone comes through here we'll catch 'em in the crossfire.'

The three men, in position, sat and waited.

CHAPTER TEN

Weeping Bear led the way into what seemed, at first sight, to be a deserted camp.

It was a small, well-hidden area, and all that was visible to show anyone had been there at all was a small pile of ash where the campfire had been.

Dismounting, Weeping Bear made a strange noise in his throat that sounded like a deep growl.

Within seconds, three fully armed Indians seemed to appear out of nowhere. Bows drawn and all aimed at Ardal.

Weeping Bear spoke to the warriors. They looked puzzled and exchanged glances, before lowering their bows.

Weeping Bear spoke at length to the three braves before turning to Ardal and speaking English.

'They understand now,' Weeping Bear told Ardal. 'We go hunt bad men, then we go see wagon train boss, OK?'

Ardal smiled his thanks and waved towards the three Indians, none of whom looked over eighteen.

'You have any weapons, apart from bows and arrows?' Ardal asked.

'No.'

'I got two spare rifles and three extra revolvers, but ammo is short,' Ardal told him.

'You would give rifles?' Weeping Bear was openly surprised.

'Sure, why not? We trust each other, don't we?' Weeping Bear spoke to his three *compadres*, who at once whooped and leaped in the air. 'What the hell did you tell them?' Ardal asked, a smile creasing his face.

'I told them about the guns,' Weeping Bear said. 'Our weapons were taken by the bluebellies, all we had left were our hunting knives. But we made tomahawks and bows.'

Ardal dismounted and untied the war-bag. 'Here, there's two Winchesters, two Colts and a Smith & Wesson. You folk know how to use them?'

'We know,' Weeping Bear answered.

'Well, let's ride,' Ardal said.

Mounting up, the five men left the camp single file, Weeping Bear leading the way, with Ardal behind him.

It was late afternoon and the sun was lowering in the west, what little heat it gave out high up in the mountains was soon lost, and the horses' breath steamed out of their nostrils as they picked their way forward.

The trail grew wide enough for Ardal to ride alongside Weeping Bear. 'Is it far?' he asked.

'No, not far. But we have to slow walk the animals, the path is too rocky. Also, where their hideout is, they have excellent – is that the word? Have a good position to defend.'

'Excellent is correct.' Ardal smiled. 'Your English is far better than you think.'

Ardal was silent for a few moments, then: 'You got a plan?'

For the first time since they had met, Weeping Bear smiled. 'Yes. I plan we don't get killed.'

'Good plan,' Ardal smiled in return.

'We will leave the horses about a quarter mile from their campsite. We must get the high ground, above their box canyon, otherwise they will cut us down like dogs.'

'You know the area well?' Ardal asked.

'Our enforced exile has made us learn many things,' Weeping Bear replied. 'We are Plains Indians, but we have had to learn the ways of the mountains to survive. If you call this surviving,' he added. There was no smile on his face now.

'I know the area,' Weeping Bear went on. 'It will mean a steep climb, and we must split into two groups, one each side of the canyon. I will show you when we get there.'

Ardal merely nodded, bowing to the Indian's superior knowledge.

They rode on in silence for the next half hour, all the while the sun lowering away. Fingers of darkness threaded their way as the higher mountains blocked its rays.

Eventually, Weeping Bear signalled a halt. They found themselves in a small clearing, water trickled down a rock face to their left. Underfoot there was grass of sorts, enough for the animals to graze on for a while at least.

'We leave the horses here,' Weeping Bear said. 'Running Elk, Eagle Eyes and Too Low Moon will take the west.' Then, looking at Ardal, 'We will take the east. Keep low and silent and wait for my signal.'

Wordlessly, the two groups split and started to climb.

Jess led the way through the mountain trail, the four men riding as hard as the terrain would allow, which at times was just a canter.

'Not far now,' Jess called back over his shoulder. They rounded the bend just before the trail widened slightly where there was a small opening to the left; the scene of Bill's death.

Slowing to a walk, Jess reined in and halted. The four men dismounted, ground-hitched their horses and drew their six-guns.

Silence.

Peering around the rocks, Jess could see nothing. No horses, and certainly no Ardal. He crept forward, his eyes darting from the rock floor to the ledge above from where they were pinned down.

Nothing.

Braver now, Jess motioned for Bert and the other two men to follow. He walked towards the rock where he and Rob and Ardal had fought off the Indians.

Again, nothing. Nothing, that is, except the leather straps that had bound the Indian. 'Damn!' Jess swore loudly.

'What it is, Jess?' Bert asked.

'The Indian we captured is gone, too!'

'Hell! What do we do now? Tracking up here ain't easy. And who took who?'

Jess walked back to where the Indian ponies had been tethered, looking for a sign.

'I can only figure whoever took off headed east,' he said more to himself than anyone in particular. 'Wouldn't make any sense heading west, towards the wagon train.'

Bert now took over. 'OK. We head east, following this trail. I want you men to keep your ears and eyes open and your rifles cocked. I don't aim to lose any more men.'

The four mounted and set off at a walk, taking care to keep as quiet as possible and scrutinizing the land for signs. Silence filled the air as they rode slowly eastwards, each man buried in his own thoughts, each man wondering if Ardal had survived – or was dead.

Clem Watkins stayed low at the far end of the box canyon. He inhaled deeply on his quirly, then ground it out with the heel of his boot.

The pervading silence told him that they had been found, but by whom? And how many? And where the hell were they?

Clem had been sure the riders would enter the canyon by the trail, which they had covered. The crossfire would cut them down before they knew what hit them. But they hadn't.

The eerie silence seemed to make the atmosphere dense, like a cloak of prairie fog rolling in.

Clem reassessed their situation: if they weren't coming in by the trail, that meant one of two things: either they'd ridden on, which was unlikely, or they were gaining high ground.

Raising his eyes, Clem peered up into the high rock wall that surrounded the canyon. Halfway up each side he could make out Marty, and on the other side, Harry, covering the entrance.

Higher up Clem tried to discern any movement, but from his vantage point at the base of the canyon, the sheer rock wall couldn't be climbed, even by a mountain goat.

Then he caught a feint flash; sunlight reflecting, on what?

Movement.

Or was it his imagination?

Eyes watering with the intensity of his stare, eyes forced wide, unblinking, Clem fixed a point high above the canyon floor, and waited.

There it was again!

No doubt in his mind now, Clem slowly raised his rifle and, picking a point 3 or 4ft ahead of the last flash, fired.

The canyon reverberated with the echo of the loud explosion of the Winchester that shattered the eerie silence.

Clem could see that his shot had hit nothing more than rock, and there was no movement up there.

'What ya see, Clem?' It was Harry who called out.

'Goddamn your ass!' Clem swore under his breath. There was no way he was replying! Harry had given his position away, the damn fool!

Shots started raining in from Clem's left. Slugs were ricochetting wildly off the rock face, and there was, as yet, no return fire.

Clem concentrated on keeping low and at the same time, trying to pinpoint the source of the shots.

He caught sight of muzzle flash; that was all he needed.

Slowly, he raised his rifle, rested it on a rock and beaded down the sight line.

He took a deep breath, licked his lips and felt a trickle of sweat course down his face as his finger slowly squeezed on the trigger.

Concentrate, you damn fool! he told himself as, slowly, he held his breath as the rifle exploded.

It seemed to take an age before he heard a muted grunt of surprise. His shot had found a target. Even as this registered, rifle fire started up from Harry's side of the canyon. But Clem could tell they were wild, random shots, fired by a man in panic.

Dang fool'll run out of ammo. Clem kept his cool and loaded another shell into the breech.

If he had hit someone, they weren't showing it. He tried desperately to listen, in between Harry's wild volleys, for any sound of their attackers, either in movement or distress. But he could hear nothing, except the constant ringing in his ears from the blasts of rifle fire.

Taking aim again, Clem sighted down the long barrel hoping for some movement – somewhere!

His thoughts erupted as a blast of fire opened up on his right. So, he thought, they plan to outflank us! Shifting his bulk around, he peered at the rock face to his right, again seeking any sign of movement. He caught sight of Marty's Stetson briefly, then raised both rifle and eyes upwards, sweeping from left to right.

There! He saw something! He tugged, rather than squeezed the trigger and his crooked grin betrayed his joy at seeing a figure rise up, arms held high and fall backwards.

Maybe two down, he though idly.

From high above, Ardal and Weeping Bear decided to concentrate on the man on the opposite side of the canyon. The lack of firepower from their compadres on the other side of the canyon gave them serious concern. Weeping Bear sent out the now familiar deep-throated growl.

Almost immediately, all gun fire stopped, and in the eerie silence that followed, Weeping Bear strained his ears to hear a reply.

One came.

A single howl, like a coyote.

Weeping Bear hung his head. 'Two are dead or wounded,' he announced solemnly. 'That was Running Elk.'

'Let's concentrate on that *hombre* below Running Elk,' Ardal said. 'The one below us is not in sight. But there's one more down on the canyon floor who seems to be doing the most damage.'

Almost on cue, the rifle from the canyon floor opened up again as Clem tried to draw a bead on another victim. This time he was unsuccessful.

Both Ardal and Weeping Bear opened fire and peppered Clem's position. Shards of rock flew every whichway, and a few cut into the puffy flesh of Clem's face, causing him to howl.

Kate Maloney had had enough.

Never a woman to sit back and let things happen,

she made up her mind to find her husband.

Having first sorted out the wagon and ensuring the two boys were well looked after, she borrowed a pony and, without letting anyone know, set off to the rear of the wagon train.

Staring straight ahead, her mind was on one thing and one thing only: finding Ardal.

Bert Henman reined in as soon as they all heard the shooting.

But the terrain didn't allow the sound to be true: the shooting seemed to be all around them, there was no way they could pinpoint it.

'Just gotta assume it's way up ahead,' he said, more to himself than anyone else.

The other three men grunted their assent.

'Come on, let's press ahead. We may get a sighting or something soon!' Digging his stirrups into the thick shaggy-haired pony, they moved on.

Ardal and Weeping Bear concentrated their fire on the opposite side of the canyon, but the only return fire was coming from the base of it.

Clem was aware of what they were doing. He was also aware that if he didn't get out soon, they'd be swamped.

If he could just make it to the rock face to his left, he knew he could make his horse.

He paused. Keeping his head low behind the rock

that sheltered him, he waited. What the hell was Harry up to? he wondered. There was no answering fire from his position. Was he dead? Wounded? Or just playing possum?

Clem decided he didn't care which it was, all he knew was, he was getting out. Right now.

He hunkered down and, moving like a sidewinder, crawled across the canyon floor, hardly daring to breathe.

Above him the shots were still ringing out. Not so many now, they seemed to be shots designed to make their target show himself or at least return fire.

Clem made it to the rock face and slowly raised himself upright. Keeping his back to the wall, he made his way to the canyon entrance, so far unseen.

'Clem!'

The voice cut through the rifle fire. Harry had spotted him and Clem could hear the panic in his voice.

A shot rang out, and as soon as it did, Clem felt a sharp pain in his right thigh. Another shot, this time it caught Clem high up near his shoulder.

'You miserable sonuvva!' Harry yelled, standing in his anger.

They were the last words he uttered as both Ardal and Weeping Bear gunned him down where he stood.

Clem, blood dripping from shoulder and leg, edged forwards. He had to make good his escape.

They'd left the horses just outside the box canyon, hidden from the main trail and with enough coarse grass to keep them happy.

Clem tore off his bandanna and tied it as tightly as he dared around his right leg. He wasn't sure if an artery had been hit, but his right boot seemed filled with blood.

His blood.

He limped on, the exit looming closer and closer, but still 100 yards away.

Clem began to think it might as well be 100 miles away!

CHAPTER ELEVEN

So as not to raise suspicion, Kate walked the pony towards the rear of the wagon train, smiling and greeting as she went. As she neared the end, Tom Bilks, a would-be settler, reined in his team and eyed her.

They had chatted before. Tom had lost his wife and, with no children, had decided to follow their dream and head west. He looked into Kate's eyes and knew damn well what her intention was.

'Best not go alone, Miz Kate,' he drawled. 'Hitch the pony and I'll turn round, two heads're better'n one.'

'I can't let you risk, . . .'

'Ain't no riskier than what you're a'plannin',' Tom replied. 'An' I ain't letting you go alone!' he winked. ''Sides, may be in need of a wagon.'

Smiling, Kate dismounted and tied the pony to the

150

wagon. It took several turns to get it around, facing the way they had come, but they set off. In the far distance, Kate thought she heard shots, but wasn't sure.

The going was slow. Approaching the mountain trail again, the horses began to lean into their harness, clouds of steam billowing from their nostrils. But the pace was steady.

Ahead, still under cover, Ardal and Weeping Bear came to a decision. Weeping Bear needed to take care of his own, it was now time for Ardal to go get the man he'd come to despise.

Weeping Bear stared long and hard at Ardal, torn between his *compadres* and the first white man not only to trust him, but whom he also trusted.

Ardal knew what the man was thinking. 'Go, Weeping Bear, take care of your men, this is my fight now.'

Smiling, Ardal grabbed Weeping Bear's hand and the two men shook hands. With a final glance at each other, they headed off in different directions.

Firing the Winchester with one hand was tricky, but Clem managed to fire, reload, and swing the rifle back up again, pinning Ardal down as he made his way along the canyon floor. Hugging the left-hand side, Clem half-walked, half-dragged himself along: escape and survival uppermost in his mind.

Clem made it to his horse, and painfully he hauled

himself into the saddle and walked the animal along the trail.

Using his good hand, he removed the bandanna from his leg and made a sling for his injured shoulder. The leg would have to look after itself.

Turning in the saddle, Clem saw a clear trail behind him, so, with a flick of the reins, he broke into a gentle trot. He knew he needed to get off the trail, but he also needed to get to the stash; he wasn't going to leave that behind.

When the echo of the last shot had faded, Ardal chanced raising his head to take a look-see.

Silence and an empty canyon greeted his fleeting glance. Then he heard the sound of hoofs on rock.

Dammit! he muttered under his breath.

Slowly, he eased himself up from his cramped position and, keeping low, hat held up and in front of him, he made his way along the treacherous trail in the wall of the canyon.

He had to get to his horse.

Straining his ears, he listened for any sound, but it was as if he was suddenly deaf. Even the wind had dropped and only silence prevailed.

Or did it?

Eyes closed, he listened. Faint, but there, the sound of iron on rock.

Ardal donned his Stetson and lost all pretence of keeping low.

Blind and deaf to all around him now, save for his footfalls along the path, Ardal made a dash for his horse. All he thought about was *an eye for an eye, a tooth for a tooth!*

Ardal made it safely down the rocky slope and paused as he hit dirt. Listening, his senses working overtime, what he didn't hear he invented, but all around was silence. He edged forwards, towards the canyon opening and his horse.

Mounting swiftly, Ardal checked his rifle and his six-gun. Fully loaded, he pulled his Stetson down hard, kicked his heels in and loped into a trot, keeping his Winchester across his lap.

The narrow trail was rocky and slippery, and soon Ardal had to slow his eager mount down to a walk.

Ahead, thinking he was out of trouble, the bleeding outlaw slumped in his saddle, keeping his horse moving using the reins and one knee. The bleeding had stopped as far as he could tell, but it seemed a lot colder than he remembered.

The campsite where they're buried their stash was not far away now; a small site in a sandy clearing between two boulders.

Clem took a circuitous route to reach the rocks, knowing that his tracks would be fresh and could be spotted by a blind man.

Falling more than dismounting, Clem landed on his back in the soft sand. The fall was still enough to wind him, and he lay there, getting his breath back, and willing the fresh bout of pain away.

This, he thought, is where it ends.

Feeling his way to his knees, Clem forced himself upright. He grabbed his rifle and saddle-bags. He was readying himself for the final shoot-out.

Tom Bilks was humming to himself in a gentle low way, Kate sat beside him, her eyes alternately sweeping left and right for any sign of her husband.

'Be a while 'fore we pick up any sign, I reckon, Miz Kate,' Bilks said in a soft voice.

'I know, Tom,' Kate answered, distractedly. 'But just in case. . . .'

Tom nodded sagely, without replying.

A shot rang out.

Tom reined to a halt to listen, but the surrounding mountains seemed to bounce the sound at him from all directions, the echoes reverberating before gradually disappearing. The silence seemed eerier, denser.

'That was close,' Kate said.

'Could be,' Tom replied, 'could be.'

Another shot, loud and clear rang out at least ten minutes after the first.

Tom waited several minutes before he got the wagon rolling again, but there were no more shots.

The only thing keeping Clem alive was the buried loot.

He'd lost a lot of blood, he knew that. He also knew if he fell asleep, he might never wake up again.

Having got his breath back, he took his arm out of the sling and tried to see what damage had been caused.

He felt as if his shoulder was on fire, stabbing pain shot down his arm as he moved it.

Peeling back his shirt, he lifted his vest top and saw the ugly crimson hole where the bullet had entered, moving his right hand across his shoulder, he felt for an exit wound.

His hand came back covered in blood. Ironically, he smiled. At least the slug wasn't inside, one less pain to endure.

He shucked himself against one of the boulders, breathing hard and sweating slightly, despite the cold wind blowing down from the mountains.

Then he saw the rider.

The man was intent on following signs, to the extent he wasn't looking anywhere but the ground.

Slowly, Clem pushed the butt of his rifle into his right shoulder. He sighted down the long barrel, figuring the rider was some 100 yards distant and, making allowance for the wind, he eased back the trigger, squeezing gently. He might only get one shot!

The explosion of the Winchester shattered the fragile silence, seconds later Clem saw, with grim satisfaction, the rider catapult from his saddle, crash

155

into the dirt and not move.

The throbbing in his shoulder and leg were almost unbearable, the recoil from the rifle seemed to affect every part of Clem's body, making him wince in pain.

But he had to move quick. He had no idea how many, if any, other men were on his trail, and he needed to get the stash loaded on to his horse and high-tail it out of these damn mountains – maybe for good, as he only had himself to consider.

He smiled to himself again, all that booty, and just for me!

Ardal flicked on eye open. The other was buried in the sand.

He was fighting for breath, and it seemed as if every ounce of air had been knocked out of him.

He moved the fingers of his right hand, saw them move, and somehow that made him feel better.

Then he tried to move.

Pain shot from his left arm and chest. Ardal thought about this: there was only one shot! He was definitely hurting in two places.

Gently, using his right arm as leverage, he eased himself over on to his back. The wounds throbbing out like drums in his temple.

To his left was a rock: shelter. He had to get shelter.

His left arm hanging uselessly, Ardal managed, unseen, to crawl behind the rock where he lay, getting his breath back and trying to figure what to do next.

Out of the corner of his eye he saw his mount wandering back towards him and at this he grinned.

'Come on, boy,' he whispered. 'Just a little closer!'

The animal pricked up his ears at the sound of Ardal's voice and he whinnied.

Coming close to Ardal, the horse nudged the man with his head. Ardal grabbed the loose reins and held on, literally for life.

The gentle whinnying of Ardal's horse made Clem look round. Painfully, he was digging into the sand to retrieve his booty. He stopped. His senses suddenly alive again.

The man Clem had shot was no longer there!

Sweat running down his face, it didn't take long for Clem to figure out where the man was. Above the rock Ardal hid behind, the horse was clearly visible.

A sneer crossed Clem's face as he raised his rifle once more.

Keeping a tight hold of the reins with his right hand, Ardal pulled himself upright. The horse, seeming to know, raised his head to help the man get to his feet.

Swaying, Ardal lunged for his rifle, before falling back into the dirt once more.

A shot rang out and the slug clipped the top of the rock before ricochetting harmlessly into the air. But it was loud and shocking enough to spook the horse, who bolted.

Ardal's lifeline vanished into the distance.

But at least he was armed. There was still a chance! And now he knew the direction of his sworn enemy.

'Shit!' Clem oathed as he saw the slug had missed. But he took some satisfaction in seeing the horse bolt.

Torn between finishing the man off and getting his loot, Clem looked first one way then the other; the loot won.

But he had to make sure.

His greed was overcome by the thought of being back-shot as he tried to make his getaway.

Digging the spade into the sand, he left it there and cocked his Winchester.

Standing on his good leg, he leant against the rock, aimed, and waited.

Sooner or later that damn critter who had been stalking him would make a mistake – a mistake that would cost him his life and Clem's freedom.

Sweat trickled down his face in rivulets as he concentrated, one eye closed, sighting down the long barrel.

Nothing but silence.

No movement.

'Damn your hide!' Clem yelled in frustration and, losing patience, loosed off three shots in quick succession.

Still no sound or movement.

Mebbe, Clem thought, I kilt him already.

So thinking, he grabbed the short-handled spade again and began digging once more. Why the hell we buried it so deep? his mind kept saying. Only the thought of an easy life, wine women and song, kept him digging. Wine, women and song. . . .

The spade hit something hard. Ditching it, Clem used his hand now to scoop out the sand. He grinned maniacally and groped for his treasure.

Ardal, his ears still ringing from the shots, pulled himself up behind the rock, using it to steady his rifle. Shards of rock had splattered all around Ardal's head, one or two piercing his face, but he hardly felt them.

He knew he had one chance, one shot. He didn't think he had the strength to stay upright for long, and if he sank down his assailant would soon finish him off, or leave him to die.

Resting the barrel of the rifle atop the rock, Ardal beaded Clem. The pain in his chest and arm seemed to intensify and the sweat was dripping from his face with the effort of concentration.

He closed his left eye, took a deep breath, took aim, and gently squeezed the trigger.

'Hush, hush now, it's all right. You're going to be all right.'

Ardal, bewildered, opened his eyes to see the smiling face of Kate above him.

159